SAM I AM

ILENE COOPER

SCHOLASTIC PRESS · NEW YORK

Library of Congress Cataloging-in-Publication Data

Cooper, Ilene
　　Sam I am / Ilene Cooper.—1st ed.
　　　　p.　cm.
　　Summary: Twelve-year-old Sam, the son of a Jewish father and Christian mother, struggles to understand religion and its role in his family's life during the Hanukkah and Christmas holidays.
　　ISBN 0-439-43967-1 (alk. paper)
　　　　　　　　　　[1. Family life—Fiction.　2. Religions—Fiction.
　　　　　　　3. Identify—Fiction. 4. Interpersonal relations—Fiction.
　　　　　　　　5. Christmas—Fiction.　6. Hanukkah—Fiction.]　I. Title.

PZ7.C7856Sam　2004
[Fic]—dc22

　　　　　　　　　　　　　　　　　　　　　　　　　2004041715
　　　　　　　10 9 8 7 6 5 4 3 2 1　　04 05 06 07

Printed in the U.S.A.　37

First edition, October 2004

The text type was set in 12-point Bembo.

Book design by Kristina Albertson

FOR DEVIKA WERTH —
THE BEST OF BOTH WORLDS

CHAPTER ONE

Looking back, everything fell apart the day the Hanukkah bush fell down. At least, that was the way it seemed to Sam.

And the morning had started off so well. Ten days without school stretched out ahead of Sam, like, well, ten days without school. Nothing to do, nothing to worry about. Oh, there was some homework, including a book from the seventh-grade reading list to finish, but all that could wait until after Christmas. Sam was a fast reader.

If being on vacation wasn't good enough, Sam had the house all to himself that morning, which hardly ever happened. He had slept late. Usually, his mother, and sometimes his father, were around when he got up on a Saturday, questioning him about what he was going to do with the day. He was almost sorry they weren't there so he could tell them, "Nothing."

A note from his parents informed him they were out shopping. Sam hoped that meant shopping for presents, not groceries. His sister, Ellen, home from her first semester at college, must have taken their little brother, Maxie, somewhere because they weren't around either.

Just a year ago, Sam had hated being home alone. He could clearly remember a miserable evening during last year's holiday vacation. His parents had gone off to a party, Maxie was at a sleepover, and Ellen was out on a date. Sam had insisted that he was old enough to stay by himself, and to his surprise his parents had agreed. He'd spent the night huddled under the covers in his parents' bed, watching a man selling baseball memorabilia on a home shopping show. Nothing really bad could happen while some guy with a bad haircut was insisting that you buy a bobble-head Willie Mays. Could it?

Sam had never confessed his fear, but he hadn't stayed alone again, either, until Pluto came to live with the Goodmans. The dog had appeared at the front porch one day in July: tired, small, and the color of Wheaties that had been soaking in milk. Everyone in the family agreed that he was adorable and that they should adopt him. Pluto, named for either the Roman god of the underworld or the Disney character, depending on whom in the family you talked to, soon grew frisky and large. Sam and Ellen, with Maxie tagging along, were pretty good about taking him for walks, so he was quickly housebroken. But then Ellen went off to college, and school started for Sam and Maxie, and that pretty much was the end of

Pluto's formal education. As Pluto grew bigger and ever more rowdy, Mr. Goodman kept insisting that someone should take "that poor, hapless mutt to obedience school," but no one ever did. Despite his lack of insight into the rules of communal living, Pluto was nothing if not good company, and while he showed no interest in being a watchdog, his impressive size probably deterred would-be burglars. That's what Sam told himself, anyway, and soon he was quite comfortable when he was home alone.

Heading into the kitchen, Sam decided to make the most of his time without questions or supervision. He fixed himself a baloney sandwich — strictly forbidden for breakfast — and headed into the family room, where the TV was all his for a change. He plopped himself down on the couch to see if the home team, Northwestern, had started its basketball game yet. Pluto wiggled next to Sam, relaxed for the moment. Before hitting the power, Sam glanced around the spacious family room, all spiffed up for the holidays: the gaily decorated tree in the corner, the cards the family had received taped around the doorways, the green-and-red striped candles on the mantel. This was nice, he thought contentedly.

He should have known it couldn't last.

Sam barely had time to click through five or six channels, looking for the game, when the doorbell rang. He got up with a groan, and headed for the living room. Suspiciously, he peered out the front window. It was just Avi.

"Hey," Sam said, opening the door.

Avi, who was almost as rambunctious as Pluto, practically tumbled through the doorway. "Hey, what's up?"

Sam liked Avi. He had moved to Evanston at the start of the school year, and it was fun to have a friend who lived right down the street. Still, Sam thought regretfully, it would have been nice to have had just a little more time to himself.

Avi followed Sam back to the couch and immediately caught sight of the untouched baloney sandwich waiting on the coffee table. His eyes darted from Sam to the sandwich, and his face wore the exact expression that Pluto's did when the dog wanted some human food.

"You hungry?" Sam asked.

"Yeah. I just got back from synagogue and I've barely had anything to eat all day." Avi was a pretty big kid. Sam wondered what constituted "barely."

"You went to synagogue on the first day of vacation?"

"My bar mitzvah is coming up. I've got to go to services and do a bunch of other stuff."

Sam pushed half his sandwich toward Avi. "I've been to bar mitzvahs," Sam said. "You have to stand up on a stage and read in Hebrew."

"You're telling me?" Avi replied glumly. "I have to conduct

the whole service, practically. I read from the Torah and talk about what it means. And I give a speech. Thanking a bunch of people." He slowly took a bite out of the sandwich.

"But you have a party, right? And you get presents?"

Avi brightened. "Yeah. It's going to be a good party, too."

"Well, there you go," Sam said encouragingly. "It will all be worth it."

"I hope so. Sometimes I get a stomachache when I think of getting up in front of all those people." Avi put his half of the sandwich down on the plate.

Sam was glad Avi was the one about to be bar mitzvahed. He knew that the Jewish coming-of-age ceremony meant you were now considered a man in the eyes of the congregation. But, to be honest, Sam didn't really feel as if he was that close to being a man.

Sam and Avi turned their attention to the Wildcats game that had just started. Sam liked football, and baseball was okay, but basketball was really his game: pretty to watch, but not too anxiety-producing — not until the last few moments, anyway. The boys were letting out a cheer for a Wildcats three-pointer when their own lusty screams and the more-distant noise of the crowd was pierced by the sound of an in-house crash. Actually, it was more like a thud, enlivened by music — a tinkling crescendo as lots of shiny balls and glass ornaments hit the wood floor along with the tree.

Sam and Avi jumped up and ran over to the corner of the family room where the once-proud evergreen had reached for the ceiling. Now, it was lying on its side, its branches a jumble of tinsel, broken ornaments, and still-blinking lights. A shaking pile of tan fur, lightly coated with pine needles, cowered near the couch.

"Wow," Avi exclaimed, impressed by the mess.

"Pluto!" Sam shouted at the dog. "What have you done?"

Pluto lifted his head and glanced sadly at Sam. *What can I say?* he seemed to ask. *It was all a horrible accident.*

Sam bent down and picked up two pieces of a candy cane ornament and then glared at Pluto. "You have totally demolished the Hanukkah bush," he said in a strangled voice.

Pluto got up and slunk into the kitchen.

"The *what?*" Avi asked.

"The Hanukkah bush," Sam replied absently. He walked gingerly around the tree, trying not to break any more ornaments. Not that there were many left intact. The tree had fallen in a way that had done maximum damage.

"Why do you call it that?"

"Huh?"

"The tree?" Avi said, gesturing to the fallen wreckage.

Sam turned his attention back to Avi. "Oh, because my dad is Jewish and Mom isn't, and she always had a Christmas tree when she was growing up, but he didn't. So when they first got married, my dad agreed to have a tree, but he said they'd have to call it —"

"The Hanukkah bush!" Mrs. Goodman stood stock-still in the doorway of the family room. "My Lord, what happened to it?" She looked accusingly at Sam.

"I didn't do it," Sam protested.

Pluto made the mistake of choosing that moment to dart back into the room and start sniffing at the broken branches.

"Was it the dog?" Mrs. Goodman marched over to Pluto and angrily pulled him away from the tree by his collar. But when she saw his hapless, *I-Know-I-Done-Wrong* expression, she softened — at least toward Pluto. "I suppose it really isn't his fault." She threw Sam an angry look.

"Well, it isn't *my* fault," Sam said indignantly.

"It is the fault of everyone in this family," Mrs. Goodman yelled. "No one has taken responsibility for this dog." Sam's mother was on a roll now. "The poor dumb creature. How can you expect him to know right from wrong, when no one takes the time to teach him anything?"

Sam pouted. Just because he happened to be in the room at the same moment Pluto galloped in, why was the dog's undisciplined personality suddenly his fault? Where was Ellen? She could at least be sharing this chewing out.

Mrs. Goodman whirled around to face Avi, who automatically shrank back. "What about you? Do you want a dog for Christmas?"

"What dog?" he squealed.

"This dog."

"No, ma'am. My mother's allergic."

"Oh, if only I had thought to say that when this mutt came to the door." She patted Pluto's head anyway. Then she moved closer to the tree and looked down at the shattered ornaments. Her face grew a little pale as she took in the scope of the damage. Slowly, she leaned over and picked up a delicate glass angel, now missing one of its wings. "I got this from my father when I was seven years old."

Sam was horrified to see tears forming in his mother's eyes. His mother hardly ever cried, and when she did, it was usually because she was happy.

Mrs. Goodman stood for a long, silent moment clutching the angel. In a flat voice, now devoid of anger, she said, "Sam, will you start cleaning this up?" Then she walked out of the room, the angel still in her hand.

Sam looked down at the mess, and then over at Avi.

"I'll help," Avi said with a sigh.

A shaken Sam headed into the kitchen. "I'll go get a garbage bag."

The holiday season was not off to a very good start.

CHAPTER TWO

Sam slipped quietly back into the house. He had spent the afternoon at Avi's watching the rest of the basketball game but had been too upset to enjoy it, even though Northwestern won by ten points.

Mr. Goodman had given Sam permission to leave. The boys were in the middle of cleaning up the debris that was once the Hanukkah bush when Sam's father had walked into the kitchen. Mrs. Goodman was putting away the groceries as tears silently rolled down her cheeks.

Mr. Goodman knew trouble when he saw it. "What's wrong?"

Out of the corner of his eye, Sam could see his mother silently gesture toward the family room.

"Oh geez," Mr. Goodman said, moving close enough to the doorway to get the full, sad picture. "What happened?" he asked, directing his question to Sam. "I drop your mother off, go get gas, and I come home to a disaster."

"Pluto knocked over the tree," Sam informed him.

Mr. Goodman shook his head. He walked over to the prone tree and surveyed the damage for a moment. Bending down, he picked up an intact ornament — a wreath made out of felt.

"I'm putting the ornaments that weren't broken in a pile," Sam said, gesturing to a pitifully small heap on the mantel.

Mr. Goodman placed the wreath on top of a rubber reindeer and a plastic Santa. "She never really liked this one," he murmured.

"Can I go to Avi's house when we're done?" Sam asked, as he shoved tinsel in the garbage bag.

"That okay with you, Avi?" Mr. Goodman asked.

Avi, who was being surprisingly meticulous in his search for unbroken ornaments, nodded.

"Look, you're almost finished, and I can lift the tree by myself. Why don't you just go?"

Sam felt a little disloyal leaving his dad to finish the cleaning and deal with his mom. On the other hand, he wanted desperately to be somewhere else for a while.

"Are you sure?" Sam asked.

Mr. Goodman reached over and rubbed Sam's hair, which was embarrassing to have done in front of Avi but felt good, anyway. "Sure."

Sam didn't know what to say to his mother, but after grabbing his jacket he ducked into the kitchen. "Uh, Mom, see you later."

"Okay, Sam." Mrs. Goodman tried out a tremulous smile. "I'm sorry I yelled. I was just — disappointed."

Sam thought "heartbroken" might be a better word, but he mumbled, "It's all right," and went across the street.

Now that he was home, Sam wanted to make sure of what he was walking into. The downstairs was deserted. The television in the family room was off, which was unusual, and without the twinkling lights of the Hanukkah bush, the cards and candles looked lost.

He took the stairs two at a time as he always did to the second floor. There were three bedrooms upstairs: one for his parents, one for him, and a small room that belonged to Maxie. When Maxie was born, the attic had been converted to a bedroom big enough for Ellen to have a dressing table, her sound equipment, and an well-worn armchair with a footstool. There was also plenty of wall space for her posters, mostly of old, dead movie stars like James Dean. When she went off to the University of Wisconsin, Sam had hoped he would inherit her room, but when he suggested a move, she had shot him a withering glance and said, "Talk to me in four years."

Even before reaching the landing, Sam could see that Maxie's bedroom was dark; he was probably upstairs with Ellen. The door to his parents' bedroom, however, was ajar. Even if it had been closed, he would have been able to hear his parents' raised voices and the word "tree."

"You never wanted a tree, anyway," Mrs. Goodman was saying. She banged a drawer shut for emphasis.

"Annie, I told you right from the start that having a Christmas tree made me feel uncomfortable. But I knew how much it meant to you."

Sam could hear his mother's loud sigh out in the hallway. "I know. It was a compromise. The Hanukkah bush."

"The name was really just a joke that stuck," Mr. Goodman said.

"The kids loved having a tree," Mrs. Goodman replied, a little belligerently.

"Sure, what kid wouldn't? I used to beg my parents for a tree when I was little."

Sam crept close enough to see his mother turn away from her dresser in surprise. "Really? You never told me that."

Mr. Goodman shrugged. "I didn't think it would help my case. But yeah, as a child I felt deprived because my non-Jewish friends had big, beautiful trees with tons of presents under them."

"So you should be happy your children grew up with a

tree." In her flannel shirt and jeans with her hair pulled back in a braid, Annie Goodman looked almost like a kid herself.

"I guess," Mr. Goodman said uncertainly. "So let's just get another one."

Mrs. Goodman shook her head no.

That surprised Sam. It hadn't occurred to him that they might not get another tree. He didn't want to be caught eavesdropping, so he quietly made his way up to the attic. Maybe Ellen knew why their mother was so set against bringing another tree into the house.

Ellen was on her bed, reading. Maxie sat next to her, watching his sister's small black-and-white TV.

"Hi," Sam said, sinking down in the worn armchair.

Ellen put her book down. "Welcome back to the house of gloom." With her dark curly hair, and a body that was more round than it was thin, Ellen looked a lot like their father. Sam was wiry like his mother and had her straight butterscotch-colored hair. Maxie was a mix. He was thin, too, but his hair was dark and without a curl in sight.

"Did you know we aren't getting another tree?" Sam demanded.

"Mom doesn't want one," Maxie said, looking away from the television.

"She thinks it just wouldn't be the same," Ellen said, recounting the conversation. "She doesn't want a tree with generic ornaments from the drugstore. Her old ones were special because she'd started collecting them when she was Maxie's age."

"She was crying," Maxie added.

"Yeah, I know," Sam said. "I saw her."

Maxie looked at Ellen. "Was she more sad, do you think? Or mad?"

Ellen considered the question. "Both. And I think a lot of things she's been holding in are starting to spill out."

Before Sam could ask his sister exactly what she meant by that particular observation, Mr. Goodman called up from the floor below. "Maxie, I'm going to get the Chinese food. Do you want to come with me?"

Maxie made a small face, but he got up. "I'll be right down."

"Tell Dad I'm with Ellen," Sam said.

Maxie nodded as he headed downstairs.

"He always does what he thinks he's supposed to. What a great kid," Ellen added fondly.

"Like me."

"No, not like you. You were a pest when you were that age."

"That's because you were twelve when I was that age," Sam retorted, "and you treated me like a pest. You're much nicer to Maxie than you ever were to me."

The Goodman children were unusually far apart in age. Their father made a joke out of it. "Your mom and I had a good idea every six years: Have a kid."

Sam didn't mind the spacing. He had plenty of friends with brothers and sisters a little older or younger, and it seemed like they were always fighting. He fought with Ellen sometimes, and she could be plenty snotty when she wanted to, but mostly she looked out for him, and she practically acted like another mother to Maxie. As for his little brother, no one could be mad at him. His mother had once called him a gentle soul, and that said it all about Maxie.

"Well, now I'm eighteen and you're still a pest, so go away."

Sam ignored the directive and kicked off his shoes. He didn't think Ellen really wanted him to leave, anyway. "So what kind of Christmas is this going to be with no tree?"

"A weird one."

"They were talking when I came up here," Sam said. "Dad said he wanted a tree when he was a kid, but I guess Grandma Sally wouldn't let him have one."

"Really," Ellen said, looking at Sam as if he had finally had something interesting to say. "Did he say anything else?"

"No. I mean, I didn't want to get caught listening, so I came up here."

His sister sat up a little straighter on the bed. "Grandma

Sally is pretty religious. I've always wondered how Dad got to be so un-Jewish."

"What do you mean? He's Jewish," Sam argued. "He says he's Jewish, and he loves all that Jewish food that Grandma Sally cooks."

"That's not what it means to be Jewish," Ellen said scornfully. "He doesn't go to synagogue, and he doesn't observe any of the holidays."

"We go to Passover dinners." They were called "seders" and Mr. Goodman's relatives always invited Sam's family to join them.

"Yes, and haven't you ever noticed how uncomfortable Dad is with all the prayers that are said at the table?"

Actually, Sam hadn't.

Ellen looked thoughtful. "And he certainly isn't interested in Christianity. I think you could say he's anti-religion."

"That's not true!" Sam wasn't sure why, but it seemed important that his father not be labeled as "anti-religion." He searched his mind for an example to bolster his opinion. "He doesn't mind if Mom goes to church. And he tells her to have a good time," he added.

"'A good time,'" Ellen repeated derisively. "Mom wants some God time, not a good time." She looked pleased with her small play on words.

All right, so maybe going to church wasn't Sam's idea of a

good time, either, but God time didn't have to be a bad time. Did it?

"Besides," Ellen continued, "she only goes to church a couple of times a year. And she almost never takes us with her. I think it's because she doesn't want to upset Dad."

"We could go if we wanted to," Sam replied uncertainly.

Ellen leaned forward. "Yes, but we usually don't. It's sort of an unspoken rule in this house: Don't talk about religion. Are you so oblivious that you haven't even noticed that?"

Sam hated when Ellen made it seem like he was Maxie's age and totally unaware of what she had started calling in high school "the nuances of life." For a while he had thought it was two words: "new ances." He had asked his mother what "ances" meant. It took her a while to figure out that he was talking about nuances; then she said it meant subtleties. He was embarrassed to tell her he wasn't 100 percent sure what that word meant, either, but his mom, like moms do, caught his puzzled expression and said, "The little things, Sam. Important things, but ones you might not notice unless you're looking closely."

Since that conversation, he had been trying to pay more attention to the nuances of life, but most of the time he had other stuff to think about, like homework and sports — and, lately, Heather Daniels. He especially liked thinking about Heather Daniels.

"Ellen, Sam," Mrs. Goodman called from downstairs. "The food will be here any minute."

"We'll be right there," Ellen yelled, swinging her legs off the bed. "Be nice to Mom," she hissed as they made their way downstairs.

"I'm always nice to Mom," Sam protested. "It's you who—"

Ellen brushed past Sam to hug Mrs. Goodman, which annoyed Sam because if anyone gave their mother a hard time, it was Ellen. Her senior year in high school, whole days had gone by without Ellen saying a civil word to her. He thought Mrs. Goodman had actually been a little relieved when Ellen left for college.

Mrs. Goodman looked surprised but pleased by her daughter's hug, even as she continued setting the table.

"I'll do that," Sam volunteered, glaring at Ellen.

"I'm almost done, but you can find the chopsticks," Mrs. Goodman said.

As Sam rummaged around the junk drawer where the chopsticks were kept, his father and Maxie stomped into the house with the Chinese takeout, shaking off white flakes.

"It's snowing," Maxie informed them enthusiastically as he hung his coat on the hook by the door.

Mrs. Goodman finally smiled one of her real smiles. "Yes, we see."

"I'm going to build a snowman tomorrow, and Sam can take me sledding . . ." Maxie looked as if he could hardly wait.

The family took their places at the table. When dinner was Chinese food, it was served out of the cartons, and it was every person for himself. Nobody needed to be told to "dig in."

"I don't know if I can do any of that stuff tomorrow, Maxie," Sam said, spearing an egg roll. "I want to go to the mall and look for Christmas presents." Then, an awful thought struck him. "We're still going to have presents, aren't we?"

"Why wouldn't we?" Mr. Goodman asked with a frown.

"Well, we don't have anyplace to put them now. . . ." Sam saw his parents exchange a glance.

"That brings up something your mother and I have been talking about," Mr. Goodman interjected.

Sam wasn't sure he wanted to hear what that was. Not if the uncomfortable conversation he had overheard upstairs had anything to do with it.

Ellen didn't hesitate, though. "Okay, what have you been talking about?"

"How we're going to spend the holidays," Mr. Goodman said. "We thought we might try something a little different this year."

Ellen brightened. "Are we going away? Mexico would be good. Or the Bahamas."

"No," Mr. Goodman said. "We're not going anywhere."

"Oh." Ellen delicately scooped up a piece of kung pao chicken with her chopsticks. "I suppose a trip was too much to hope for."

"This is going to be a weird holiday," Sam commented.

"Different," Mrs. Goodman corrected him. But her lips were a bit twisted as she pushed out the word.

Maxie stopped eating. He was very good at noticing when something was amiss, and just as good at worrying about it.

"Okay," Mr. Goodman began, "we all feel bad about the tree falling down, but since it's gone, and your mother doesn't want another one, I thought we might make some new traditions this year."

Three pairs of young eyes looked at their father suspiciously.

"We always try to light the candles at Hanukkah time," he continued, "but let's face it, usually we forget. This year, though, Hanukkah begins on Christmas Eve, so we can celebrate both holidays at the same time. The lighted candles can be our decoration."

The response from the Goodman children was underwhelming.

"Can you do that?" Sam asked, separating the green onions from the lobster sauce and moving them to one side of his plate. "Celebrate Christmas with Hanukkah lights?"

Mr. Goodman frowned. "Celebrate the spirit of both holidays is what I meant."

The only sound in the room was that of chewing.

Finally, Ellen said, "Maybe we should think more about going somewhere. I know it's late, but sometimes there are cancellations. Like on cruise ships."

"Unfortunately, Ellen, the high cost of a college education means we won't be going on a cruise," Mrs. Goodman replied. She glanced at future college students Sam and Maxie. "Or anywhere else in the foreseeable future."

Maxie had a more immediate concern. "But where are we going to put the presents?"

His parents thought about it. "We can put them next to the menorah," Mrs. Goodman suggested.

"What's the menorah?" Maxie asked.

"You remember. That's the name for the candleholder," Mr. Goodman said.

Maxie slid off his chair and leaned against his father. "Tell me the story of Hanukkah."

"I thought you knew it."

"I forgot."

Mr. Goodman put Maxie on his lap. "A long time ago —"
Mr. Goodman began.

"How long?" Maxie interrupted.

"More than two thousand years ago."

"That *is* a long time," Maxie agreed.

"Anyway, the Jewish people were being persecuted, but a group of rebels called the Maccabees were fighting back. It was a great day for the Maccabees when they recaptured the holy temple in Jerusalem. But when they went inside, they were shocked. The temple was supposed to be clean and pure, but the soldiers of the opposing army had done terrible things to it."

"Like what?" Maxie asked, eyes wide.

Ellen remembered this part. "The temple was filthy, and they had poured pig's blood on the altar."

"Yuck," Maxie said.

"And put up statues of Roman gods," Mr. Goodman added. "So the Maccabees scrubbed the temple and put in a new altar. There was a menorah in the temple that was supposed to burn constantly, but there was no holy oil left to light it. Finally, one vial of oil was found. It was barely enough to last one day, but they lit the menorah, and do you know what?"

"What?" Maxie responded.

"The flame burned for eight days, until new oil arrived, and the temple was restored."

"So it was a miracle," Maxie said, impressed.

"That's what they say," Mr. Goodman replied.

Ellen shook her head. "There's no such thing as a miracle —"

"Now, wait a minute —" Mrs. Goodman interrupted.

"A miracle is a supernatural happening," Ellen continued, reaching for another helping of chicken lo mein. "It's when God intervenes in the affairs of man."

Mr. Goodman looked warily at his daughter. "How do you know so much about miracles all of a sudden?"

"I saw a show on the Discovery Channel. Most things people think are miracles have very logical explanations." Ellen looked at her father and raised one eyebrow. It was her special expression that said, *I know more than you and I'm about to prove it.* "If you believe in miracles," she continued, "you have to believe in a God that makes the miracle happen, right?"

"I guess so," said Mr. Goodman.

"Do you believe in God?" she pressed, pointing her chopsticks at her father.

Sam leaned forward to listen for the answer.

Mr. Goodman suddenly seemed very interested in his fried rice. "Well, I'm not sure."

Ellen nodded sagely. "There you are. No God, no miracles."

An unmiraculous silence fell upon the kitchen.

God. Sam hadn't really done much thinking about Him one way or the other. Considering how important He was supposed to be, He was surprisingly easy to ignore. Sam thought back. He supposed when he was little, he had believed in God, though in sort of the same way he believed in Santa Claus — someone who decided if you were good enough to get the things you asked for. It had been years since he had asked either God or Santa for anything, and he no longer wanted "stuff" as much as good grades, a place on the school basketball team, a smile from Heather Daniels. He got the grades because he studied hard. Perhaps he should rethink and ask God for some much-needed help with basketball and Heather.

Maxie broke into the quiet with soft words. "I believe in God," he said. "And miracles."

"Well, good, Maxie," Mrs. Goodman said, standing up to get some more napkins. "Good for you."

"But, Maxie —" Ellen began.

"Leave him be, Ellen. There's nothing wrong with a little belief," Mr. Goodman said. He sounded like he might be trying to convince himself. "Everyone should believe in something."

Sam wasn't sure how he felt about God, but he knew one thing he had always believed in: the Hanukkah bush. A pretty, fragrant Hanukkah bush that looked like a bit of fairyland had come to life in their family room. A Hanukkah bush hung with his mother's ornaments, the spun-glass angel, the red-and-white candy cane, the tiny gingerbread house she had bought on a trip to Switzerland when she was eighteen. But this year, there would be no Hanukkah bush and none of the familiar, sentimental things that adorned its branches. He missed it already.

CHAPTER THREE

"Are you watching the news?" Mrs. Goodman asked Sam, not bothering to hide the surprise in her voice.

Sam turned to his mother. A commercial had just come on, so he wouldn't miss anything. "Yep. Homework."

His mother sat down on the couch next to him. "What kind of homework?"

"Current events. Do you do current events with your classes?" Sam asked. Mrs. Goodman had gone back to work after Maxie started school full-time. She taught the fourth grade.

"Not as much as I should," Mrs. Goodman said thought-fully. "What's your assignment?"

"I'm supposed to find stories that show how different countries celebrate the holidays."

"And what have you found out so far?"

"They fight." Sam didn't mind working on current events assignments as a rule. But he wasn't enjoying this one. He had expected stories on TV or in the newspapers about how

Father Christmas rather than Santa visited the children of England, or what kinds of presents people exchanged in Latin America. There were some stories like that, but mostly what Sam noticed as he clicked away on the remote control was that people seemed to use the holidays as a reason to argue about one thing or another.

Mrs. Goodman looked at Sam with troubled blue eyes, very much like his own. "What do you mean, they fight?"

"Well, Bethlehem, where Jesus was born?" Sam began.

His mother nodded.

"There's all kinds of fighting there. Palestinians and Israelis. And there's some kind of march going on in Northern Ireland. Protestants against Catholics, I think."

"Those fights have been going on for a long time," Mrs. Goodman said.

"And right here in Chicago, some parents don't want their kids to sing Christmas carols because they're not Christian."

Mrs. Goodman sighed. "Happy holidays, hey Sam?"

"Yeah, right."

His mother got up. "I've got some phone calls to make. Let me know when you start writing your assignment. We can talk about it."

Sam didn't really want to talk about it. The whole thing was kind of depressing. But there was one question he had for his mother. "Mom?"

Mrs. Goodman turned back toward Sam. "What, honey?"

"Why are there so many religions? And why are people always fighting about them?"

His mother shook her head. "I don't know, Sam. You'll have to ask God about that."

Sam leaned back against the couch, thinking. Pluto liked that position because it made a bigger lap for him to jump on, which he promptly did. Sam stroked Pluto's head, and the dog closed his eyes, a dreamy expression on his face. Sam realized that he had always known his mother believed in God in a way that his father didn't. He had even heard her say that she talked to Him, so he supposed that he shouldn't be surprised that she thought people could ask God questions. But did she really think He gave answers, especially to big questions like why there were so many religions in the world? And if He did, why would those answers go to a twelve-year-old nobody like Sam Goodman?

Pluto opened his eyes, jumped off the couch with a hearty enthusiasm, and started chewing up one of the sneakers that Sam had kicked off before he put his feet up on the coffee table.

"Hey, hey," Sam yelled, "stop it!" Pluto gave Sam the *Make-Me* look. Was this what God had to put up with? Sam wondered. People who did whatever they wanted and, when God told them to stop, just looked up at Him and said, "Make me"?

Sam tugged the shoe out of Pluto's mouth, and immediately the dog went for the other one.

Grabbing the other shoe, Sam said, "Come on, Pluto. You're going in the basement because you can't behave." That's what a neighbor had told the Goodmans worked with her dog. God could take a lesson here, Sam thought as he put on his teeth-dented shoes and got up. Pluto followed him unwittingly downstairs and was shocked to see the gate close behind him. "Sorry, Buddy, time-out," Sam informed Pluto. A couple of countries also needed a major time-out, it seemed to Sam. Why didn't God give it to them?

As he clumped back upstairs, Sam thought maybe he'd start his current events paper now, while all his observations about holiday "celebrations" were still fresh in his mind.

But as he sat at the small wooden desk in his room, notebook opened, pen at the ready, his mind drifted off to the question of religions. There were so many of them. He ticked off some that came immediately to mind: Judaism, Christianity, Islam, Hinduism, Buddhism. He was sure there were more. That meant there were a lot of people believing in a lot of different things. Sam's curiosity was sparked. Maybe he *should* ask someone about how there could be so many different ways to think about religion. Reviewing his choices, he decided on Ellen. True, depending on her mood, she was only marginally more likely to answer him than God, but she had mentioned she was taking a comparative religions class, and she had already tussled with choosing a religion. For a while last year she'd proclaimed she was a Buddhist. Sam wasn't sure what that entailed other than burning incense in her room, which, as Mr. Goodman had noted, "stunk up the house."

Sam didn't mind putting aside his homework. He climbed the stairs to Ellen's room, where he found her sitting in her chair, working on the laptop computer she had been given as a graduation present.

"What are you doing?" he asked.

Ellen didn't bother turning around. "E-mailing."

Sam walked around the room, looking at all the bottles and jars on her dresser. Then there were hair things and jewelry and other doodads scattered about. Girls had so much stuff. He wondered if Heather had a lot of stuff. He didn't think she wore any makeup, because she always looked like she had just washed her face; it was all fresh and shiny. He preferred a girl to look like that, not like some of those singers on MTV, with too much makeup, always sticking their navels in somebody's face. In the past, when he'd heard Ellen say some guy wasn't her type, he hadn't exactly known what she meant. Now he did. Those MTV girls weren't his type. Heather was.

Sam tried to figure out just how he was going to interrupt Ellen, when she turned around and looked at him. "I'm glad you're here."

"You are?" Sam said. This was a first.

Ellen nodded. "We've got to come up with a plan."

"A plan for what?"

She gave her patented exaggerated sigh. "Even you must have noticed, Sam, that this holiday season is getting all screwed up. The 'new traditions' idea doesn't sound promising. Not unless we do something about it."

Sam agreed. "The tree is a goner, and who knows what else is going to disappear."

Maxie appeared in the doorway as if he sensed an important conversation was taking place. "I like the menorah," he said. Mrs. Goodman had gone out and purchased a new menorah. It was shiny silver.

"It's not about the menorah, Maxie." Ellen motioned him into the room. "It's about making sure that this holiday isn't a total bust."

"So what are we supposed to do about it?" Sam asked, flopping down on his sister's bed.

"Take your shoes off if you're going to get on my bed," Ellen ordered.

"I just put them on," Sam protested, but he kicked them off anyway.

"First," Ellen continued, "we have to make sure we get Mom something nice. She's still feeling really rotten about the ornaments."

"Then why don't we get her some more?" Maxie suggested. He climbed on the bed next to Sam, after carefully removing his shoes.

"Okay, that's a good idea," Ellen replied. "We can pool our money and get her a couple of very special ornaments."

"What money?" Sam asked.

"Hey, Scrooge, you've got plenty of money."

"It's in the bank," Sam protested.

"In your piggy bank," Ellen responded scornfully. "Break it open."

"It's got a key," Sam replied, defeated.

"I don't have any money," Maxie said, picking up one of Ellen's stuffed animals.

"Ask Dad. He'll give you some. And we should all make sure that we go out of our way to act nice on Christmas Day."

"Nice!" Sam fairly shrieked the word. "There you go again. Maxie and me are always nice. You're the one who fought with Mom all last year."

"This is just the kind of thing I'm talking about," Ellen said haughtily. "I don't want you yelling and starting arguments."

"Fine, I'll be *nice*." The room was getting a little stifling. Sam was ready to go. His questions could wait until later.

"Then it's all decided," Ellen said. "We're going to have a lovely holiday. Whatever it is."

But the chances of the holiday celebration turning out to be lovely took a turn south when the Goodman children heard their parents' news the next day.

They were sitting around the dining room table. Mr. Goodman insisted that the family have dinner together twice a week. That usually dwindled down to once a week, and they had already had Chinese takeout. But with Ellen home, Mr. and Mrs. Goodman said the family should have dinner together whenever they could. Tonight Mrs. Goodman had enticed everyone with spaghetti and meatballs, all the kids' favorite. Sam loved slurping the spaghetti, especially when it caused Ellen to make a face like she was going to be sick.

"You sound like a vacuum cleaner," she remarked with disgust.

Sam slurped once more.

"Sam!" Now Mr. Goodman was getting annoyed.

Mrs. Goodman handed Sam the basket of garlic bread. "Here, it's quieter."

Sam laughed, causing some bits of chewed meatballs to come out of his mouth.

"Ohh, gross!" giggled Maxie.

Sam leaned over and let Pluto slobber him with kisses, thus effectively removing all remnants of food from his face.

Sam wiped his face with his napkin. He could fight with

Ellen and tease Maxie, and chafe under his parents' rules, but being a part of the Goodman family was pretty easy.

Then came the bombshell.

"Kids, your mother and I have invited both of your grandmothers to spend this Friday with us. It's Christmas Eve and the first night of Hanukkah."

"You're *kidding*," Ellen screeched. The news was so shocking, she almost knocked over her water.

"Grandma Sally and Nana?" Maxie said wonderingly. "I thought they don't like each other."

Trust Maxie to state things clearly and simply. Sam knew a little bit of the story. When his parents had gotten married, neither one of his grandmothers had been happy. It was because of the religion thing. Both of his grandfathers were long dead, and Sam wondered if things would have been different if they had been alive when his parents got engaged. But they weren't, and his grandmothers had made a huge fuss over the wedding. Nana, his mom's mother, wanted his parents to get married in the Episcopal church. Grandma Sally wanted them to get married in a synagogue. Each of his grandmothers said she would die of embarrassment if her son/daughter was married by a priest/rabbi.

His parents had wound up getting married by a justice of the peace, with just a few of their friends in attendance. Neither grandmother came to the wedding. Since then, as far as Sam knew, Nana and Grandma Sally had been in the Goodman house together only for birthday parties, and then they had sat on opposite sides of the room, barely acknowledging each other. The kids saw a lot of both of their grandmothers, just not at the same time.

"Why did you invite the *grandmothers*?" Ellen asked her parents, distress tingeing her voice. "Sam, Maxie, and I were going to try to make it a nice day."

"There's no reason why it shouldn't be nice," Mr. Goodman said mildly.

"I talked to Nana," Mrs. Goodman said, "and your dad talked to Grandma, and we explained that, with both holidays falling on the same night, this would be a good time to bury some hatchets and try to celebrate together."

Sam shoved some more spaghetti into his mouth, but somehow it didn't taste the same.

"I think it's a good idea," Maxie said.

"You do?" his mother said with delight. Clearly, she wasn't sensing the same response from her two older children.

"Well," Maxie began, "Christmas and Hanukkah are nice holidays, so maybe Grandma and Nana will feel like being nice, too."

"From the mouths of babes," Mr. Goodman said, ruffling Maxie's hair.

Sam and Ellen exchanged looks. Only a babe could be as

hopeful as Maxie. A babe, or parents with their heads in the sand.

"So you told them this would be a good time to celebrate together," Ellen interrupted. "What did they say?" she asked ominously.

His parents exchanged glances.

"They both promised they would come," Mrs. Goodman finally said.

"To celebrate?" Ellen raised one eyebrow in disbelief.

"I think they'll try to be on their best behavior," Mr. Goodman replied optimistically.

There was trying, and then there was doing, Sam thought. Would they try? Maybe. Do? That remained to be seen.

CHAPTER FOUR

Even though everything about the holidays was different this year, one thing that remained the same was the rush. It seemed like every few hours someone needed to go to some store or other: for presents, wrapping paper, groceries. But there was one place Sam didn't mind going, and that was to the mall. He knew that some people thought malls were tacky and plastic, but he didn't agree. He thought malls were terrific, especially Red Oak, the mall closest to his house. Bad weather, bad mood, it didn't matter once you were inside the mall; and you didn't need much money to have a good time — maybe just enough for a McDonald's burger and fries. But the best part was that you never felt lonely at the mall, because there was always someone to hang out with. If you were really lucky, Heather Daniels might be one of those people. That made for the best mall experience of all.

Not that Sam couldn't see Heather in school. She was in his seventh-grade homeroom, where she sat kitty-corner from him. She was in a couple of his other classes as well. But

Heather was very picky about who got her attention, and she never spoke to him in school. She never really talked to him at the mall, either. However, at the mall, kids from the seventh and eighth grades were always goofing around, and Heather might say a few words to Sam in passing. Those offhand remarks were what kept Sam's hopes up.

There was only one part of the mall experience that Sam wasn't crazy about: getting a ride to Red Oak from his father. His dad was a lawyer and almost always had to go into the office on weekends. So usually, he was the one who dropped Sam off. Sam figured that his father must have read an article that advised parents to use the time they spent in cars with their children as an opportunity to *Talk*. Mr. Goodman regularly tried to bring up some serious topic he felt needed discussing on the fifteen-minute ride to the mall.

Even now, months later, Sam could feel his stomach tighten as he thought about the ride last summer when his father began talking about sex.

He should have known something was up. His father called him Son twice before they hit the first stoplight. Sam had learned over the years that when his dad cleared his throat and called him Son, he was going to say something that Sam didn't want to hear.

But *sex,* for crying out loud? It wasn't as if his mother hadn't read him *Where Did I Come From?* at least five times when he was little. After the initial reading, she'd turned to him and sweetly asked, "So, Sam, now do you know where you come from?"

Before Sam could answer, Ellen had bounded into the room yelling, "The orphanage! Sam came from the orphanage, and we're giving him back!" Sam had cried copious tears, so maybe that's why Mrs. Goodman thought she needed to read the book three more times. When she was pregnant with Maxie, she'd read it again for good measure.

The information had been repeated in fifth-grade health class. Sam wasn't quite sure what health had to do with anything, but there had been plenty of visuals and lots of talk about what was normal. True, nothing about sex seemed very normal when Coach Helprin was discussing it, but between *Where Did I Come From?* and health class, Sam felt he knew more than enough. So why his father thought he had to add his two cents to the topic, Sam couldn't say. But that hot, muggy, August day, Mr. Goodman cleared his throat, called Sam Son, and launched into a discussion of sex versus love and how to tell the difference.

Sam was sure he would remember those fifteen minutes as among the longest in his life. When his father was finished, Sam didn't know which of them was sweating more, and it wasn't from the heat. Sam liked his dad, but he liked him best when he was goofing around or taking him to a Cubs game, not when he was trying so hard to be a *Father.* Besides, Sam didn't have the heart to mention that he was having trouble getting girls to just talk to him. It would be a long time before he needed to know the difference between sex and love.

By December, Sam had let his guard down because most of their car conversations since the summer had centered around the Cubs and how lousy they were, and then about the Bears and how lousy they were. But on this Christmas Eve morning, on the way to the mall to shop for last-minute presents, Sam had heard the rumble of Mr. Goodman clearing his throat, and he knew a serious discussion loomed.

"Sam," Mr. Goodman began.

Sam slunk down in his seat.

"I think we should talk about this holiday thing."

"It's too late to change now," Sam said. "Hanukkah, not Christmas. Menorah, not tree."

"Yes, I guess that's the short version. But Mom and I are both a little worried you kids are feeling deprived this year." Mr. Goodman took his eyes off the road long enough to glance over at Sam. "Are you?"

Should he be honest? Sam wondered. It was always such a crapshoot with parents. They invariably said, "You can talk to us about anything," and then when you told them something they didn't want to hear, they got all crumply and sad looking, like a cigarette stubbed out on the curb.

"We've talked about it, Dad. Me, Ellen, and Maxie, we're going to try to make the day nice," Sam said reassuringly. Still, why shouldn't his father know the things that were bothering him? "It's just that . . . well, the holidays won't be the same."

To Sam's surprise, Mr. Goodman chose to take that particular statement as a positive. "That's right, Sam, they won't. You've got it. We're trying something a little different here, and it sure won't be the same, but maybe it will be better."

"How?" Sam asked. Personally, he didn't see it.

"For one thing, this new arrangement might add a little more religion to the holiday season. Even when we had the Hanukkah bush up, we never really did anything to observe either holiday."

Sam remembered Ellen's comment, that Mr. Goodman was "anti-religion." Gingerly, he asked, "So if you want to celebrate Hanukkah, that means you're not against religion, right?"

Mr. Goodman looked at Sam as if he had poked him with a stick. "Why would you ask that?"

Aaargh! Sam knew he shouldn't have gone there. "I don't know . . . you just never seemed that interested in Judaism or Christianity. Now, you want us to light the Hanukkah candles."

"Organized religion doesn't appeal to me much," Mr. Goodman responded stiffly, "but I do like some of the holidays, some of the traditions of Judaism."

Sam couldn't help himself. He pushed forward. "Okay, but what about Mom's traditions? Should we do some of those?"

"The tree was her tradition, and we did it for many years," Mr. Goodman said, his voice remaining tight. "She doesn't want to have one this year, so we're going to put a little more emphasis on Hanukkah."

"Mom goes to church sometimes."

His father turned into the mall parking lot.

"Maybe we should all go to a Christmas service or something," Sam pressed.

Mr. Goodman didn't say anything but he seemed startled by Sam's suggestion.

Now look what you've done, Sam said to himself. He began backpedaling. "Hey, Dad, don't worry about religion. We have our own traditions, you know. We always watch the Grinch, and we rent it if it isn't on television. We watch lots of those holiday shows."

Mr. Goodman frowned as he waited behind a car that was waiting for another car to pull out of a parking space. "Watching TV is not observing a holiday, Sam. Television isn't real life, you know."

Sam thought in many ways it was better. But he was smart enough to know that particular insight wasn't what his father wanted to hear. He tried frantically to think of something to say that would make him feel better.

"Hey Dad, you know how when I'm worried about a test or a dentist appointment you always say, 'It's only one day. You'll get through it'?"

Mr. Goodman nodded.

"Well, Hanukkah is only eight days, so we'll get through it."

His father's smile was weak at best.

Sam hurried out of the car and didn't look back. He was eager to forget the question of Christmas versus Hanukkah, and it was forgotten as soon as he walked through the heavy glass doors of the mall, even though the whole place was decked out with fake greenery and giant presents, festively wrapped, stacked about as decorations.

Maybe it was the Christmas spirit, or maybe it was just his lucky day, but the first person Sam saw as he passed the food court — in all her perfect blondness — was Heather Daniels. And she spoke.

"Sam."

Sam had never noticed his name was so short and snappy. Sam! Great name!

"Oh hi, Heather." Trying for casual, Sam feared he'd meandered into barely audible.

"You're friends with Jeremy Marcos, right?" she asked.

Sam had to stop himself from crossing his fingers and holding them up to show Heather just how close he and Jeremy were. "Uh, sure."

"Good. I have to buy Jeremy a present, and I don't know what to get him."

Why was Heather getting Jeremy a present? Sam didn't know how to pose the question without sounding nosy.

As if he had asked it, anyway, Heather said, "It's not my idea. Our parents are friends, and we're spending Christmas Eve at Jeremy's house. My mother thought it would be nice if I picked out Jeremy's present." Heather's rosebud lips formed a little pout.

"You don't want to pick out a present for Jeremy?" Sam asked tentatively.

"How would I know what to get Jeremy?" Heather replied crisply. "Could there be any less likely recipient for my largesse?" the question implied.

"So you want me to help?" Sam asked. He hoped that's what Heather was getting at.

Heather's pout turned into a smile. "Yes, I do. Will you?"

Would he ever! Sam nodded.

"All right, let's go get something."

Like gerbils on a wheel, they picked up the pace, moving briskly around the mall. Moving even more quickly were Sam's thoughts: She wanted him to help her! But where should they go to buy a present? What sort of present should he suggest? Surely he ought to be making conversation with Heather, but what about?

He realized happily that Heather didn't seem to notice that he had become mute.

"This is so dumb," she said, shaking her head as they pushed their way through the crowds. "I hope Jeremy's mother isn't making him pick out a present for me. And if he is, I hope he asks a girl to help him, like you're helping me."

Sam greeted that statement with a tremulous smile.

"Say, my mother gave me twenty dollars. Do you think we can get something for ten?"

"Probably," Sam said, with more confidence than he felt.

"Good," Heather responded with satisfaction. She leaned so close to Sam, he could inhale the delicious fruity scent of her hair. "I saw a pair of earrings I want to buy with the change."

His mother would kill him if he did something like that, Sam thought, but it was none of his business what Heather did with the leftover money. Now, though, his burden rested even more heavily on his shoulders. Not only did he have to find a present for Jeremy, he felt obligated to make sure Heather got her earrings.

"So what are you doing over vacation?" Heather asked.

"Not much." What a witty answer, Sam thought miserably.

"We were supposed to go skiing." There was that pout again. It was adorable! "My sister got the flu. Very convenient since she hates skiing," Heather added darkly.

"Do you think she's faking?"

"No. She's hacking and sneezing her germs all over the place. I hope she's miserable. I hate my sister."

Hate, Sam thought. That seemed a little strong. "Well, maybe something fun to do will come up here."

"Like what?" Heather asked skeptically.

Before Sam had to find an answer to that loaded question, inspiration struck in the gift department. They were passing a store called Knowledge College. The name was stupid, but the shop stocked all sorts of interesting things: games, puzzles, books, videos. Sam wouldn't mind a present from there himself.

"Well, here we are," Sam said, stopping so fast in front of Knowledge College that Heather almost barreled into him.

Heather looked at Sam quizzically. "Doesn't this store have educational stuff?" She used the same disdainful tone for the word "educational" as she had for "Jeremy."

"No, well, some of it, but there's a lot of cool stuff in here." Sam felt suddenly protective of Knowledge College.

"Okay," Heather said with a shrug.

"We'll get something really good," Sam promised as they walked into the busy store. Sam looked around at the shelves groaning with merchandise. Now that he was here, he didn't know where to begin.

Heather picked up a wire mesh gizmo decorated with shiny beads that you could manipulate into different shapes. "This is fun," she said.

For about two minutes, Sam thought, his heart sinking.

"What do you think?" Heather asked, her big blue eyes questioning. She glanced at the price tag. "It's only eight dollars," she added happily.

Sam cleared his throat. "I think he might like something else better."

Heather frowned. "Like what?"

Uh-oh. Sam glanced around wildly. "He'd like a video game better. They're not that expensive," he added quickly.

"Well, we certainly want Jeremy to have something he likes," Heather said sarcastically as she reluctantly put the wire thing down.

Sam moved to the video game shelves and nervously scanned the titles as Heather stood beside him and watched. "What about this?" he asked, pulling one down. It was a game called Buried Treasure, and the description on the back of the box made it seem pretty intense: pirates, sea monsters, wild animals. He handed it to Heather, who barely glanced at it. She handed it back to him. "How much?"

Sam found the price tag. "12.99. Plus tax."

Heather sighed as she saw the hope of the new earrings fading away. She pulled some money out of her purse. "Okay."

"That's it?" Sam said with surprise.

"I had to get a present. Now I've got one," Heather said.

Grabbing back Buried Treasure, she marched over to the cashier, Sam trailing in her wake.

"Jeremy likes reading about buried treasure and stuff."

"Uh-huh," was Heather's only response as she made her purchase.

"Well, thanks, Sam," Heather said, walking toward the door.

That was it? Sam and Heather's Excellent Adventure, finished so abruptly? At least she had said his name again. "You're welcome," Sam called after her, but he doubted if Heather heard him. She was already out in the mall.

Only by radar did Sam find his way to the food court. His mind was focused on going over every detail of his encounter with Heather. He had actually helped Heather Daniels with a chore she had to perform. Good. She had picked him out of the milling crowds to do her bidding. Better. She had not seemed inclined to linger once the purchase was made, however. . . .

"Whoa, Sam!"

Sam snapped back to reality. Sitting at a table were Avi and Jeremy eating fries and drinking Cokes as if it were lunchtime, not 10:30 in the morning. Now that Heather was gone, Jeremy was just the person Sam wanted to see.

Sam sat down and helped himself to some of Avi's fries.

"Hey, get your own," Avi protested. But Sam just gulped them down.

Choking a little, he said, "Hey, Jeremy, I know what one of your Christmas gifts is."

Jeremy looked at Sam suspiciously. "How would you know something like that?"

Avi looked worried. "We're not giving each other presents, are we? Because I really don't have any money to buy —"

"No, doofus, we're not giving each other presents." Sam shook his head.

"So what am I getting? And who from?" Jeremy demanded.

"It's from a girl."

Avi made a little "ooh" sound, but Jeremy just shrugged and said, "Heather Daniels."

"You know?" Sam said with surprise.

"Yes. We're going over there tonight, and Heather and I were supposed to pick out each other's presents. But I'm not buying anything for Heather. Nobody can make me."

"Well, I just saw what Heather bought you."

"Something stupid, I bet."

Sam was offended for Buried Treasure. "No, it wasn't."

"I don't care. I don't like Heather Daniels."

"Why not?" Sam asked with surprise. He just assumed everyone thought Heather was as neat as he did.

"She thinks she's so perfect," Jeremy informed him.

Avi looked up from his fries. "She's mean. Haven't you noticed?"

It was true that Heather divided the seventh-grade girls into three categories: her friends, her enemies (you didn't want to be one of those), and everyone else, as little noticed as dust. But mean? Well, there was the time Ruth Edison had cried after getting a D in English, and Heather nicknamed her Baby Ruth, making her cry all the harder.

Sam shrugged. "Lots of people can be mean."

Avi took a long drink of Coke and then let out an enormous burp. "But she's so good at it."

She hadn't been mean to him as they'd shopped for Jeremy's present, Sam thought. She had almost been nice. And so pretty. Hadn't Avi and Jeremy ever noticed the way Heather's long blond hair curled slightly at the ends, and her body, which really was a Body? Glancing over at his friends, who were now blowing the wrappers off straws, Sam decided perhaps they were too immature to appreciate Heather. Just because she didn't like everyone who walked the halls at Hamilton Junior High, was that such a crime? At the moment, she seemed to like him. Who knew what might develop? Sam was not going to let two burping, wrapper-blowing dorks like Avi and Jeremy ruin his good mood. As far as Sam was concerned, today was the day he had stuck his foot into the slightly open door to Heather Daniels's heart.

CHAPTER FIVE

Sam would have been happy to spend the rest of the morning in the food court on the off chance that Heather might wander by looking for him. But with one present left to buy and knowing that his father would be waiting to pick him up outside the mall in precisely an hour, Sam said good-bye to his friends and headed off once more to battle the holiday shoppers, though without Heather at his side, it was a far lonelier task.

As Ellen had noted, Sam was something of a skinflint, but once he'd handed over a fair chunk of his savings for his mother's ornaments, in the spirit of the season, he decided to spend a little more and buy better gifts than his usual offerings. Since his sister liked James Dean, he had bought her a DVD of the movie *East of Eden*. For Maxie, he got an official major-league baseball. His father was tricky to buy for, but last night he'd come up with an idea. Mr. Goodman was a Beatles fan, so Sam decided to buy him a CD to replace an old scratchy Beatles album his father still played. After that task was completed successfully, it occurred to Sam he should buy something for his grandmothers.

He tried to push the thought away. The mall was jammed with people, none of whom happened to be Heather, he was tired, and he had spent almost all his money. But the generous impulse still clung to him and so he pressed on.

Of course, good intentions aside, there was the problem of what exactly to buy. He thought about his grandmothers. They were about as different as they could be, except for the fact that they were both old, older than a lot of grandmothers. Nana had been young when her first child, Sam's uncle Jerry, who lived in California, was born. But she was almost forty when his mom came along. His father was Grandma Sally's only child. She had been pretty old when he was born, too. So the grandmothers had their age in common. Other than that, nothing.

Nana was tall, taller than his dad, and delicately thin. Her hair, fine and white, was usually pushed back with a velvet headband, and she almost always wore skirts or dresses; no pants, unless she was gardening or fishing. Nana spoke when she had something to say, and much of the time she and Sam spent together didn't require talking. She had taught him how to fish and had tried to teach him how to play the piano without much success. But Sam loved listening to Nana play because she did it so beautifully.

Grandma Sally, she talked constantly. Maxie once said he had gotten an earache after a phone conversation with her. But she didn't just talk about herself. She was always interested in what her grandchildren were doing, and she handed out plenty of smart advice that ranged from how to deal with parents to how to properly deal a deck of cards. Unlike Nana, Sam wasn't sure that Grandma Sally owned a dress. Running suits were her favorite outfits, which amused Sam because she was too heavy to actually run anywhere; Grandma Sally always said that she put on weight one tablespoon at a time, tasting everything that she made. She was as generous with hugs and kisses as with her delicious food, but sometimes you just had to wriggle away from her embraces. Along with all those kisses came lots of five- and ten-dollar bills, and for someone who was as appreciative of money as Sam, her gifts were extremely welcome.

They were as different as pickles from poodles, but Sam liked spending time with both of his grandmothers. Just not together.

Full of good intentions, Sam wandered into first one store, then another, trying to find something, anything, his grandmothers might like. Perfume? He didn't have a clue what their preferences were. Music? Nana liked classical; Grandma Sally listened to singers he'd never heard of, whose names he couldn't remember. Clothes? Out of the question. He went into jewelry stores and walked right out again. Ready to give up, Sam paused as he passed a candy store. Everybody liked candy, he thought to himself. The sweet smell drew him inside.

"Can I help you?" the teenage clerk behind the counter asked Sam.

"I'd like two boxes of candy."

The girl snickered. "Great. You've come to the right place. What kind of candy?"

Sam looked around and realized he was faced with an astounding array of choices. There were chocolates, of course, and jellies, mints, chocolate-covered pretzels, and fudge. Alternatively, there were nuts.

The salesgirl looked at Sam impatiently. "Should I help somebody else?"

"No, no." If she left, he'd probably just walk out. Then he spied a display of candy boxes behind the counter. They weren't very big, but some of them were wrapped in paper decorated with little Santa Clauses and others were wrapped in paper that sported Jewish stars. Perfect.

"I'll take one of those and one of those," he said, pointing at the boxes. It took the rest of Sam's money to pay for them, but at least he had succeeded in his quest.

Walking out of the store, Sam felt good. So often, his father complained that his older son didn't follow through on things. And this, he had to admit, was true. Whether it was cleaning his room or finishing a report for school, Sam was very likely to leave the job half finished. Well, no one could accuse him of not following through on his holiday shopping. Parents, sister, brother accounted for. He had even bought his grandmothers presents, something they would surely like, and best of all the candy was already wrapped.

Trust Ellen to try to weasel in on his foresight and sensitivity, Sam thought with resentment. He had put his candy on the living room coffee table with the menorah and the rest of the presents, just a half hour or so before the two grandmothers were supposed to arrive. Ellen was shocked when she saw the two gaily wrapped boxes, clearly chagrined that she hadn't thought of it first and embarrassed that her grandmothers would be getting a gift from only one young Goodman.

"Sam," Ellen began earnestly, "we're *all* grandchildren. You've got to put my name on the candy, too. And Maxie's, of course."

"No way," Sam said, snatching the boxes of candy back off the table.

"Why not?" his sister countered.

"Because I thought of it!"

Ellen tried flattery. "That's right, you did. And it was really great of you to come up with the idea and then actually buy something."

Sam nodded, but clutched the presents more tightly.

Then she tried guilt. "I was so busy picking out just the right ornaments for Mom, ones that she will cherish, just the way she loved the old ornaments Pluto broke while you were in charge of him, that I didn't have time to think of buying presents for Grandma Sally and Nana."

"Hmmm," was all Sam said.

Bribery. "Of course, I'll be glad to put in some money for the candy. And Dad will put in some for Maxie. The money might even cover the whole cost for you."

Sam didn't hate the idea of building his savings back up.

Ellen pried the presents out of Sam's hands. "Just like I thought. You didn't remember to buy cards for these. No one will know who they're for — or from — unless you put cards on them. I have some very nice cards upstairs. Shall I get them?"

Sam nodded, defeated. It was very hard to win an argument with his sister.

Ellen had just put the candy, which now sported cards that said, "With Love from Your Grandchildren," back on the table when Mr. Goodman's car pulled into the driveway. He had gone to pick up his mother. Nana had her own car.

Mrs. Goodman hurried out of the kitchen. She was wearing the sweater decorated with little Santa Clauses that she usually saved for Christmas morning. Sam thought she looked very nice, except for the flour that was smeared on her cheek. He took the towel out of her hand and wiped the smudge off her face.

"Thanks, Sam," she said, patting him on the shoulder. She looked him over. "I'm glad you put on your new shirt."

Sam had been hoping to save his crisp, khaki shirt for some time when Heather Daniels might be around. There was a dance at the community center on New Year's Eve, but he wasn't sure if he was going or if Heather would be there to see him if he did. So, knowing it would please his mother, he had decided to sacrifice his shirt for the "holiday get-together," as his parents had started calling this evening, and hoped that new clothes would be among his presents.

"Sammy!" Grandma Sally burst into the house, with Mr. Goodman right behind her. She hurried over to him and gave him one of her signature noisy kisses on his cheek. "How are you, darling?"

"Fine, Grandma."

"Hello, Annie," Grandma Sally said, turning toward Mrs.

Goodman. They gave each other an awkward hug. "Where are Ellen and Maxie?"

Before Mrs. Goodman could answer, Grandma called out, "Maxie, Ellen, your *bubbe* is here." Grandma Sally put special emphasis on the Yiddish word for "grandmother."

Mr. Goodman, who was carrying a big covered casserole dish, said, "Annie, my mother made a kugel."

Sam brightened. His grandmother's apple kugel — a noodle pudding — was delicious.

Mrs. Goodman didn't look quite as excited. "Sally, we're having fondue tonight. I'm not sure —"

Grandma Sally frowned. "Fondue?"

"You know, Mom," Mr. Goodman interrupted. "Melted cheese and then you stab hunks of different sorts of bread in it —"

"I certainly know what fondue is, David," Grandma Sally said huffily. "But cheese and bread for holiday dinner?" She made it sound like beanies and wienies.

"It's a very elegant dish, Sally," Mrs. Goodman said stiffly.

"Oh, I'm sure it is, but Annie, it's not very . . . hearty."

Mrs. Goodman tried again. "I'm just not sure kugel and fondue go together."

Grandma Sally shook her head and smiled. "Annie darling, kugel goes with everything." She turned to Sam. "And you love my kugel, don't you?"

Sam looked at his grandmother, then back at his mother. What was the right answer to this question? "I do, Grandma, but —"

"It's fine, Sally. I'll be happy to serve the kugel," Mrs. Goodman said, taking the dish from her husband.

"And I'm sure we'll all enjoy it," Grandma Sally responded with a pleased nod. As soon as Mrs. Goodman was back in the kitchen, she turned to her son and whispered, *"Fondue?"*

"Mom, it's Annie's specialty."

Grandma Sally shrugged. "Who knew? I don't get invited to dinner here that often."

"Sam, go get your sister and brother," Mr. Goodman directed.

Sam didn't have to be told twice.

Ellen was in Maxie's room, combing his hair. "Who's here?" she asked Sam.

"Grandma Sally."

"How's it going?"

Sam shook his head.

"She's only been here two minutes," Maxie exclaimed.

Sam didn't have the heart to tell Maxie that two minutes was plenty of time to tell that it was going to be a long evening. "We'd better get downstairs."

They trooped into the living room, where there were more hugs and smacking kisses from Grandma Sally. Ellen smiled through them politely, but Maxie got on his grandmother's lap and leaned his head against her shoulder.

"This is my boy," Grandma Sally said, smiling gently down on him. "Isn't he beautiful?"

"Boys aren't beautiful," Maxie said, but he didn't look as if he minded the compliment.

The doorbell made a loud, intrusive sound. "I'll get it," Ellen said.

In the doorway stood Nana, bundled up in a pink coat with fur on the cuffs and around the collar. She pulled a luggage cart behind her, piled with presents. "Merry Christmas, Ellen. Merry Christmas, everyone." She glanced over at Grandma Sally with Maxie curled up in her lap. "Hello, Sally."

Grandma Sally gave her small smile. "Happy Hanukkah, Jane."

"Let me take your coat, Jane," Mr. Goodman said hurriedly. "Wow, look at all those presents."

This was the wrong topic to bring up, albeit an unavoidable one, since the beautifully decorated gifts needed to be taken off the cart. While Mr. Goodman unstrapped the presents, Nana launched into the subject of The Tree.

"Yes, well, I was up until midnight last night wrapping them," Nana said as she took off her coat and carefully balled her gloves into her pocket and folded her scarf. "It took a lot of effort, but I felt I had to do a special job, if only to make up for the lack of a tree. I was devastated when Ann told me about the tree. And the ornaments! She still hasn't gotten over it," Nana confided as she came into the living room and took a seat in the big wing chair next to the fireplace. Warming her hands, she continued, "Sam, why don't you help your father bring in the gifts. Of course, what are gifts without a fragrant, trimmed Christmas tree to put them under. . . ."

At that moment, Pluto, who had supposedly been locked in the basement, wandered into the room.

"Come here, you darling dog," Grandma Sally said.

Drawn to her cooing tone, Pluto trotted over to Grandma Sally, who patted him on the head. "You're a good dog, yes you are."

"I thought you didn't like dogs," Maxie said, looking up at her wonderingly. "You always said you were a cat person."

Grandma Sally looked embarrassed. "Well, yes, I like cats, but this dog is a nice dog."

Good going, Pluto, Sam commented silently. All it took to make a friend of Grandma was demolishing our Hanukkah bush.

Ever on the move, Pluto padded over to Nana, who ignored him. "So, children, how have you been?"

Ellen, Sam, and Maxie, all sensing the tension in the room, jumped into the conversation.

"I'm thinking about joining a sorority, Nana," Ellen said.

Maxie got off Grandma Sally's lap and sat down, legs crossed on the floor next to his other grandmother's chair. "I'm doing really good in reading, Nana, I've already gone through the first reader."

Nana smiled down at Maxie. "That's lovely, Maxie."

Sam tried to think of something he could say. His grades were fine, but nothing to brag about, and he had been cut from the seventh-grade basketball team. Suddenly he heard himself say, "I'm going to a dance on New Year's Eve."

"Really? How nice," Nana said.

"You're going to a dance?" Ellen asked.

Sam wished he could bite off his tongue. Just a half hour ago, he was still thinking it over. He didn't even want to go unless he knew for sure that Heather was going to be there. But now, he had committed himself, in front of his family, no less.

"A dance! Terrific, Sam. I remember my first dance," Mr. Goodman said nostalgically. "It was great. I won a dance contest, remember, Mom?"

Grandma Sally nodded. "It was at the synagogue. You went with a lovely girl. Rachel Blitzstein. Did you know she's a rabbi now?"

"You've told me." Mr. Goodman suddenly looked deflated. He seemed finished with the subject of his first dance.

"Perhaps I should go in and see if Ann needs any help," Nana said, rising out of her chair.

"It's only fondue," Grandma Sally said.

Nana glared at Grandma Sally. "I taught Ann how to make cheese fondue."

"Taught? How hard could it be? It's bread. And cheese."

"*Mother,*" Mr. Goodman said with exasperation, "I thought you weren't going to cause trouble."

Grandma Sally pasted a look of hurt and amazement on her face. "What did I do?"

Mr. Goodman shook his head. "Never mind." He got up and went over to the CD player. "What should we put on?"

"One of the Christmas CDs, of course," Ellen said.

"Can I pick?" Maxie asked. "Please?"

"I thought we were here to celebrate Hanukkah," Grandma Sally protested.

"Both holidays. I told you, Mom, *both* holidays," Mr. Goodman said.

"But aren't you going to light the Hanukkah candles?" Grandma Sally asked.

"Of course." Mr. Goodman looked at his watch. "We're going to light them any minute."

"And you're going to celebrate Hanukkah by lighting the candles while Bing Crosby sings 'White Christmas'?"

Everyone silently agreed that Grandma Sally had a point.

"Well, maybe we'll hear some music later," Mr. Goodman conceded, turning away from the CD player.

Mrs. Goodman came out of the kitchen. "Hi, Mom," she said, going over and hugging Nana. "Dinner is just about ready."

"We're going to light the candles first," her husband said.

"Oh," Mrs. Goodman said. "Fine."

The Goodmans and Grandma Sally got up and stood around the table that held the silver menorah with its nine branches surrounding a Star of David. Nana stayed in her chair but looked interested. In any case, she wasn't frowning.

"Maxie," Mr. Goodman instructed, "I'll light the shammes first, and then you can light the candle for the first night."

"What's the shammes?" Maxie asked.

"That's the candle we use to light the others."

One red candle had already been placed in the menorah. Mr. Goodman took a blue candle out of the box and started to light it with a match.

"Aren't you going to say the prayer?" Grandma Sally asked.

"Sure. I think I remember it," Mr. Goodman said. He began, *"Baruch Atoy Adonai . . ."* As he recited the short prayer in Hebrew, he gave Maxie the blue candle, now aflame, to light the red one. Maxie excitedly took the shammes and carefully brought it to the red candle's wick.

When Mr. Goodman was finished, he and Grandma Sally said, "Amen." Ellen and Sam hastily said, "Amen," too.

"Let's eat, shall we," Nana said, "before everything gets cold."

"The fondue can't get cold," Maxie informed her. "There's a little candle under the fondue dish that keeps it warm."

"I know dear. It's just a figure of speech."

Sam, aware that things were pretty icy already, tried to think of safe subjects to talk about at dinner. So did everyone else in the Goodman family. As they ate their salad and used their special metal fondue forks to spear hunks of bread and dip them in the creamy cheese, they talked about the weather, and how there hadn't been any real snow to speak of. Ellen mentioned that she was going into Chicago to see the *Nutcracker* ballet with a friend. Mrs. Goodman told everyone that she had decided to take a Chinese cooking class in January. But the only real warmth came from the tiny candle under the fondue dish.

Nana and Grandma Sally said very little — until Grandma Sally noticed that her kugel wasn't on the table.

"Annie, you forgot to put the kugel out."

"Oh, I'm sorry, Sally," Mrs. Goodman said. She beat a hasty retreat to the kitchen to get it.

"What is kugel?" Nana asked.

"Noodle pudding with raisins and apple," Grandma Sally said.

"It sounds heavy," Nana said, daintily dabbing her lips.

Grandma Sally's eyes narrowed. "Heavy?"

"Difficult to digest."

Mr. Goodman cut in. "The kids love it, Jane."

"Adults love it, too," Grandma Sally said. "At least all the adults I know."

Mrs. Goodman brought the kugel in and set it on the table. "Who would like a piece?" she asked. Everyone except Nana said they would.

"Did Ann ask you to make this noodle pudding?" Nana asked Grandma Sally.

"No, Mother, I didn't," Mrs. Goodman said, "but it's a special treat."

Nana shrugged. "For Christmas dinner, I like to make a mince pie. I would have made a mince pie if you'd asked."

"I have chocolate chiffon pie for dessert," Mrs. Goodman told her mother.

"Besides, this isn't a Christmas dinner," Grandma Sally reminded Nana as she cut herself a large piece of kugel. "It's dinner on the first night of Hanukkah."

"It's Christmas Eve as well. And when Annie was little, we always had mince pie," Nana repeated.

"When David was little, we always had kugel."

The two grandmothers glared at each other.

No one else was happy, either. Mrs. Goodman stabbed a piece of her kugel like she wanted to kill it, and Maxie seemed ready to slide under the table like he used to do when he was little and wanted to escape. Ellen, who was sitting next to Sam, muttered, "The next time we have a Hanukkah bush, would you keep a closer eye on Pluto?"

"It wasn't my fault," an indignant Sam hissed back.

"Please. Could we just enjoy this dinner?" Mr. Goodman pleaded.

Nana speared another piece of fondue. "Everything is lovely, Ann. You're a marvelous cook."

Grandma Sally settled back in her chair. "Who's not enjoying?"

I'm not, Sam thought. I'm not.

CHAPTER
SIX

Sam kicked his covers and rolled over once more. This was the worst Christmas Eve ever. When he was little, Christmas Eve meant not being able to sleep because he was waiting up for Santa. It was fun tossing and turning, listening for reindeer paws on the roof. Now, he just wanted to fall asleep so visions of this evening could stop dancing in his head.

Opening the presents, which should have been the most fun part of the evening, had started off surprisingly well. During dessert, it seemed as if Nana and Grandma Sally were ready for a truce, or perhaps they were just getting tired. Neither of them liked to stay up late, something Ellen pointed out as a potential bond when Nana yawned. There was a cordial, albeit brief, discussion of sleep habits, and while eating the chocolate chiffon pie they had even shared a few happy memories of Bing Crosby on the radio, Bing having at last been allowed to croon carols in the background. So there was every reason to be hopeful as the Goodmans headed into the living room to unwrap their gifts.

The family had decided to forgo the tradition of opening presents in the morning, so that they could all exchange Christmas/Hanukkah gifts with the grandmothers present. Sam was happy with his haul. He had gotten a lot of cool stuff from his family, including a couple of video games, some clothes, and a special gift from his father: tickets to a Bulls game for just the two of them. His presents had been a big hit, too. Ellen had even liked her James Dean DVD. She thanked him twice.

But when it came time to open the grandmothers' presents, the bickering had started all over again.

Grandma Sally had gone first. "For you, darlings," she said, opening her large black purse and drawing out three cream-colored envelopes with the young Goodmans' names on them. While duly issuing their thanks, Ellen, Sam, and Maxie had ripped open their envelopes. Inside each was money, lots of it. Sam liked getting money. It meant he could buy whatever he wanted with it, and Grandma Sally had given him enough to buy something special, with some left over to rebuild his depleted savings. After some thank-you kisses, Grandma Sally told everyone it was a holiday tradition to give children Hanukkah *gelt,* the Yiddish word for "money."

That comment had prompted Nana to speak up. Money was such an impersonal gift, she'd said. It meant that you hadn't really thought about the person you were giving to and what they might like to receive. Then she passed out her own extravagantly wrapped presents.

Grandma Sally was left steaming. "Giving money is *tradition*," she muttered as Ellen, Sam, and Maxie carefully took the ribbons and bows off Nana's presents.

Ellen received a pretty little cross on a silver chain. Grandma Sally started drumming her fingertips on the table next to her as Ellen tried it on. The drumming got louder as Maxie began leafing through his picture book version of the New Testament. "Oh, here's the Baby Jesus," he said as he held up a picture of the Nativity scene for everyone to see.

Slowly, Sam opened his gift. It was a key chain with the initials WWJD engraved on them.

"Do you know what it stands for, Sam?" Nana asked.

"Uh-huh. What Would Jesus Do."

"How do you know that, Sam?" Mrs. Goodman asked with surprise.

"Some of the girls at school wear WWJD bracelets. When you're in some kind of tricky situation, you're supposed to ask yourself what Jesus would do if it was happening to Him."

"Exactly right, Sam," Nana said with delight.

There was just one problem, Sam thought. He had no idea what Jesus would do in any given situation, say, for instance, this one.

Finally, Grandma Sally could hold her tongue no longer. "What are you trying to do?" she asked Nana. "Convert these children to Christianity on the first night of Hanukkah?"

"Convert?" Nana responded, her voice slightly shrill. "Their mother is Episcopalian. They are already half Christian."

"And half Jewish!" Grandma Sally said defiantly.

Maxie looked as if he was about to burst into tears.

"All right, that's it!" Mr. Goodman said, slapping his hands together. "Mom, do you want to go home? I can take you home right now."

Sam was amazed. This is exactly what his father used to say to him when he was little and acting up away from the house.

Grandma Sally looked as if she was tempted to say yes, but then she realized that would leave Nana alone with the three potential converts. "No, of course I don't want to go home." Grandma Sally took a deep breath and turned to Mrs. Goodman. "I'm sorry for any upset, Annie."

"That's all right, Sally." She gave her own mother a very hard look, and Nana mumbled a curt, "Sorry."

More coffee was served, and a few remaining presents were opened, but conversation was limited to polite comments about those gifts and the merits of regular coffee versus de-caffeinated. The grandmothers couldn't even agree on that. Nana said coffee with caffeine gave her heartburn, while Grandma Sally thought decaffeinated tasted like dirty laundry water. Sam's boxes of candy, which had seemed such a good idea in the store, now mocked him with their cheery wrappers representing Christmas and Hanukkah. Both grandmothers had acted pleased when he handed them out, but Sam couldn't help feeling that the last thing the Goodman family needed was something else that pointed up the family's differences.

As he kicked off his covers and sat up a little, Sam wondered yet again what it was about religion that made people want to fight with one another. This time, however, the question was personal. Disagreements in other countries was one thing. Arguments in your own living room was another. Eyes wide open, he decided maybe he should do what his mother suggested: Ask God.

He looked up at the ceiling for a while. Could you do that, just ask God a question? There was no law against it. No guarantee there would be an answer, either. Sam hesitated. Who was he to bother God? But, what the heck, he was here and couldn't sleep. God was supposed to be everywhere. Nothing ventured —

So Sam cleared his throat and positioned his body a little straighter; without realizing it, he clasped his hands. "So, God, ah, dear God . . ." "Dear God" sounded better. More like a prayer, although, to be technical, this was an informational question rather than a prayer. Still, it couldn't hurt to add a "dear" in there.

"Okay, dear God, what I want to know is, why can't people practicing different religions get along?"

Sam relaxed a little and waited for his answer as the moments ticked by. He realized this was a big question — huge, even. Certainly not a question that could be answered in a sentence or two. But he expected more than the thick silence that surrounded the bed. He closed his eyes. Maybe pitch darkness would help him hear an answer better.

Nothing.

Perhaps he wasn't listening in the right way, Sam reasoned. Eyes now open, he idled away a few moments considering how God might choose to answer him. Sam realized he had been waiting for a big, booming here-comes-the-Lord voice, but why should God expend all that energy on one kid in bed? Maybe God would sound more like that quiet voice inside you, the one he'd heard people talk about. Or maybe He just communicated through ESP, transferring His important thoughts to human beings' imperfect minds.

Sam closed his eyes again to better listen for Important Thoughts.

Of course, Sam reasoned, as he opened his eyes again, God was busy. Probably too busy to answer questions from twelve-year-olds, at least on demand. But really, he was getting a great big zero here. Nada. Zip. Couldn't God give him a crumb? Maybe just a message like "I'll get back to you as soon as I can"?

Sam flopped over on his side. It wasn't all that late. The festivities had ended about ten, Nana had left, a tight-lipped Mr. Goodman had taken Grandma Sally home, and all anyone wanted to do after that was go to his and her respective rooms. His mother, rubbing her head, gave them each a kiss, asked Ellen to put Maxie to bed, and said she had to find some aspirin. Now, it seemed like he'd been in his stuffy room suffocating under crumpled blankets for hours, even though the blinking clock told him it was not yet midnight. Sam decided to get out of bed and see if anyone else was up.

Maxie's door was ajar, and Sam could hear his soft snores. Poor Maxie. This is how little kids get disillusioned, Sam thought. He'd be warier the next time he was told how nice an event was going to be. The door to his parents' room was firmly shut and so was the door to Ellen's attic room. Then Sam looked down the stairway and noticed a light in the kitchen.

Sam padded downstairs and found his sister and Pluto enjoying some of Grandma Sally's leftover kugel. Well, there was one thing his grandmother was right about: Anytime was a good time for kugel.

Pluto heard Sam first, but he was so busy snarfing down

crumbs of the raisin-filled pudding, he barely looked up. Ellen noticed him a few beats later and motioned Sam over with her fork. "Pull up a chair."

First Sam got his own fork and plate, and then sat down across from his sister. "So that could have gone better," he remarked without preamble as he hacked off a piece of kugel.

"You think?" Ellen replied sarcastically. "Of course inviting the two grandmothers was a totally lame idea to begin with."

"Who do you think was worse?" Sam asked.

Ellen considered the question. "Well, Grandma Sally's cheap shots at the fondue didn't exactly get things off to an ecumenical start." Ellen looked over at Sam. "That means the bringing together of different faiths."

"Yeah, the evening wasn't," he stumbled over his sister's word, "whatever you just said."

"On the other hand," Ellen continued, "giving Hanukkah *gelt* is traditional. I don't know why Nana had to be so snarky about that."

"What about Nana's presents?" Sam began. "She must have known they were going to make Grandma Sally angry."

"I kind of like my cross," Ellen said.

"What am I supposed to do with a key chain?" Sam groused. "We keep the key under the window box. I think I would rather have gotten Maxie's New Testament."

"It did have nice pictures," Ellen agreed.

"Have you ever read it? The New Testament, I mean?"

Ellen shrugged. "Yes and no. I've read parts of it in the comparative religions class I took this semester, and I read a lot about the Bible. And the holy books of other religions, too."

"Comparative religions. So that's where you compare different religions?" Sam asked.

His sister rolled her eyes. "Sharp, Sherlock."

"Well, excuse me for not knowing your fancy college terms for stuff," Sam huffed.

Ellen's expression softened. "You're right. Now I'm being as bad as the grandmas, taking stuff out on you. I guess I'm just worried."

"About what?"

"How all of this religion stuff is affecting the family. Mom and Dad were arguing again after he got home. Behind closed doors, of course."

Sam could feel the kugel congealing into a tight little pudding ball in the pit of his stomach. "Could you hear what they were saying?"

"Not the words. They just sounded mad and unhappy."

Pluto came over and put his head on Sam's lap. It was almost as if he were apologizing for starting all the trouble. But if what Ellen had told him was right, this religion stuff had been a problem before Pluto ever got near the Hanukkah bush.

"You don't think they'd get a divorce, do you?"

Ellen tried to look reassuring. "No. After all, they've been two different religions the whole time they've known each other. There must have been other times when it was an issue and they didn't get divorced."

That made Sam feel a little better. Ellen was pretty smart — and she had taken that comparative religions course. Sam had a thought: If God wasn't answering his questions, maybe it was time to ask Ellen.

"So, El, why are there so many different religions?"

His sister looked at him, surprised. "That's a big question, Sam. I guess because different groups of people want to worship in their own way."

"Yeah, so why don't they just do that?"

"What do you mean? They do."

Sam tried to get his thoughts straight in his own mind so he could explain to Ellen just what he was getting at. "People, at least a lot of people, don't just worship in their own way. They're like Nana and Grandma Sally, trying to make other people think they're doing it the wrong way. What's up with that?"

Ellen looked at her brother with delight. "Sam, you're *thinking!*"

Sam was embarrassed and indignant at the same time. "I think all the time, Ellen." This was true. Perhaps his thoughts

were not always the most important, but he was thinking —
about something or another — all day long.

"Sorry." Ellen got up to rinse off her fork and dish. "The
answer to your question, I guess, is that it's important to some
people that they are right. Right about religion. And how can
they be right, if other people are doing it differently? So they
have to tell everyone else that they are doing it wrong. Give
me your plate."

Sam got up and handed over his plate and took one final
lick off his fork. "So who is right? Right about religion, I
mean."

"That's for you to decide for yourself."

"Well, what do you think?" Sam asked.

Ellen put her arm around Sam's shoulder as she turned off
the light and led him out of the kitchen, with Pluto following right behind. "Sam, as soon as I figure it out, you'll be the
first to know."

CHAPTER SEVEN

Sam awoke Christmas morning not knowing what to expect. Since all the presents had already been opened, he'd decided to sleep in. Usually he was up before his dad, and certainly Ellen, but he couldn't remember the last time he had slept later than his mother. She was the early bird, who liked getting things done before the rest of them awoke. He sniffed the air as he came downstairs to see what was cooking. He didn't smell a thing.

Ellen, still in her pajamas and robe, was curled up on the family room couch engrossed in *Rudolph the Red-nosed Reindeer* on TV.

"Why are you watching this?" Sam asked, joining her.

"Because it's on," Ellen replied with a sigh, not taking her eyes from the screen.

Sam sat beside his sister, watching for a while, afraid to ask her to at least change the channel and see if there was a football game on. "Where are Mom and Dad?"

"Still sleeping, I guess."

"Maxie?"

As if on cue, Maxie came into the family room. He was half dressed in jeans and a pajama top. He peered at the television set. "Is that Rudolph?"

Ellen nodded. "Want to watch it with me?"

Maxie shook his head. "I'm too old for Rudolph. Aren't you?"

"Not today," Ellen replied.

Sam made room for Maxie on the couch, which made it crowded or cozy, depending on your point of view. Ellen frowned as she moved over, so Sam figured she was thinking crowded.

Sam put his arm around Maxie. "I'm sorry we don't have any presents for you to open this morning."

Maxie shrugged. "When it's Hanukkah, you open the presents at night, so it's okay."

They watched Rudolph for a while. As usual, he was having problems; all the other reindeer were calling him names and wouldn't let him join in any reindeer games. Sam spaced out on the show and began thinking about last night's one-sided conversation with God. Okay, so He hadn't answered. But that didn't mean He never would.

Then Sam had a thought. If God was as smart as everyone said He was, He should use modern technology, like television, to communicate with people. You know, God, Sam informed Him silently, You really ought to go on TV. Broadcast to everyone around the world at the exact same time and say something like, "Hey folks, about that religion thing? I'm coming down on the side of the Jews." Or the Christians. Or whoever. Sam started getting excited about this idea. If You did that, he pointed out, all the fighting could stop. Everybody would know the right religion to follow.

Or would they? Would even watching God on television satisfy people if He didn't give the answers they expected? Sam could see it all now. The religions that weren't chosen would come up with some excuse about how maybe that wasn't God on TV after all. Maybe it was the Devil, trying to trick people into believing the wrong thing. Those talking heads on news shows who were always arguing about politics would switch over to arguing about religion and whether God meant what He said until viewers' heads started swimming. Deflated, Sam decided that even a full-fledged address to the universe by God Almighty probably wouldn't resolve anything.

Maxie, bored with the reindeer, turned to Sam and said, "Maybe I should wake up Mommy and Daddy?"

"No need for that, Maxie," said Mr. Goodman, appearing in the family room, a book under his arm. "We're up."

"Where's Mom?" Sam asked.

"Just combing her hair."

"Want some coffee?" Ellen asked, lifting her mug. "I made some."

"You did?" Mr. Goodman asked with surprise.

"A little something I learned at college."

"Well, I'm glad we're getting our money's worth from that university," Mr. Goodman said, walking into the kitchen to pour himself a cup. He came back with his coffee, sat down, and opened his book. Sam checked out the title. It was called *Twilight of the Gods.*

"Is your book about religion?" Sam asked him. Everything else in the Goodman house seemed to be.

"Actually, it's about the music of the Beatles," Mr. Goodman told him.

"Oh. Like they were the gods of music?"

"Something like that," he said as he began reading.

Sam and Ellen looked at each other. Their father was almost always in a jovial mood in the morning, and he never missed an opportunity to put in a plug for his favorite band, even singing a few Beatles songs off-key when the topic came up. The fact that he wasn't even humming underscored that this morning was all wrong.

Mrs. Goodman came into the room, and Sam was surprised to see that she was wearing a dress and her pearl earrings.

"Mom?" Ellen said inquiringly.

"Merry Christmas, everyone. I thought I'd go to church. Does anyone want to come with me?" Mrs. Goodman asked with what could only be described as a hopeful look on her face.

There was a brief silence. Then Ellen shrugged. "I guess I will."

Maxie nodded. "Okay."

Sam looked over at his father. Mr. Goodman wasn't volunteering to go to church. Sam wished he would. Not that he ever had before, but then they could all be together. His dad was just fiddling with his book, though, not making a move to go anywhere.

Sam couldn't see everyone trooping off, leaving his father alone. "I'll stay with Dad," Sam said, looking at his mother, not his father. He hoped he hadn't hurt her feelings.

Mrs. Goodman seemed to understand his quandary. "That's a good idea, Sam. When we get home, we'll all go out to lunch like we planned. I've made a reservation at Seaside. How does that sound, everybody?"

Everybody dutifully agreed that sounded fine.

Ellen and Maxie got up to get dressed for church.

"Has anyone taken Pluto out?" Mrs. Goodman inquired.

"I let him out when I got up," Ellen said as she headed upstairs.

"Sam, maybe you can take him out for a walk while we're gone," his mother requested.

After the others left, Sam turned off Rudolph and watched a football game for a while. He asked his father, who alternated between leafing through his book, keeping an eye on the game, and staring off into space, if he wanted to join him walking Pluto.

Mr. Goodman shook his head. "No, you go. I'm reading."

Once again, Sam felt torn. He was supposed to be staying home to keep his father company, but Mr. Goodman hadn't said three words since they'd been alone.

Sam gave it another try. "I can take Pluto for a walk later, if you want."

"No, go ahead," Mr. Goodman said, not even looking up.

Angrily, Sam went to the closet and put on his jacket. Fine, he thought to himself. Stay here, what do I care? "C'mere, Pluto," Sam called, rummaging in the closet for the leash as Pluto pranced around, eager to go out. Sam supposed even a dog would want to get away from the bad vibes in this house.

Outside, it was cold and crisp with a sprinkling of snow on the ground, just right for Christmas morning. As Sam walked Pluto down the street, he noticed how many houses had Christmas trees in their windows. If he got a little closer, he was sure he could peer in the windows and see excited kids opening their presents. He put his head down. Who needed to see that?

"Hey, Sam!"

Sam looked up. Avi was in his front yard, pulling his little sister on her sled, trying to make the most of the inch or so of snow. With a small wave, Sam pulled Pluto over toward Avi.

"Okay, Miriam, let's give it a rest," Avi said to his little sister, who was four.

Miriam stubbornly shook her head.

"We can have hot chocolate if we go in," Avi tempted her.

Miriam looked torn.

"With cookies."

Miriam got up off the sled. She walked over and gave Pluto a pat.

"She got the sled for Hanukkah," Avi explained, "but she doesn't understand that it's kind of useless without enough snow. Why don't you come in for a while?"

"What about Pluto?"

Hearing his name, Pluto started wagging his tale at a furious pace.

"We can put him in the dog run," Avi said. "We won't be gone too long." The Cohens didn't own a dog, so the narrow run beside their house was a perfect place for Pluto to wait.

Avi's house smelled great and was mad with activity. Mr.

and Mrs. Cohen greeted Sam, but Mrs. Cohen kept on grating potatoes and Mr. Cohen was busy wrapping presents. Avi's twin sisters, who were ten and always giggled when Sam was around, were setting a long table.

"We're having a Hanukkah party tonight," Avi explained. "All the relatives."

"I just finished the strudel. Now, I'm making potato latkes," Mrs. Cohen said. "Have you ever had them?"

Sam had had them at his grandmother's house. They were like crispy pancakes. "Sure."

"Do you prefer sour cream or applesauce?" Mr. Cohen asked with mock severity. "That's a big debate in this house."

"Just say both," Avi advised as he swiped a piece of the strudel from the counter where it was cooling.

"Maybe you can come by later and have some," Mrs. Cohen said as she swatted at Avi's hand.

"Yeah, my cousins will be here, and we play the dreidel game, it'll be fun," Avi added.

The dreidel was like a top. You spun it and won money or candy if your Hebrew letter came up. "Isn't the dreidel game for little kids?" Sam asked, gesturing toward Avi's sisters.

"Not around here," Mr. Cohen said, rubbing his hands together. "The stakes can get pretty high. We play double or nothing dreidel in this house."

"I'll try to come by," Sam said politely. It did sound like

fun, but he had probably had enough of family gatherings, even if the families were getting along.

"Do you want some hot chocolate?" Avi asked as he made Miriam's drink in the microwave.

As a matter of fact, Sam did. He'd had nothing to eat this morning. Ellen and Maxie had grabbed some cereal before leaving, but Sam had lost his appetite. Now, the smell of freshly baked strudel was getting to him, but he didn't have the nerve to ask for a piece since they were for the Hanukkah party. "Yeah, hot chocolate would be great. Then I've got to finish walking Pluto."

"I'll nuke yours in a paper cup. Mine, too, then I'll walk with you for a while."

"Just for a little while," Mrs. Cohen said. "There's still a lot to do."

Avi hadn't even taken off his coat, so once the hot chocolate was ready, it was easy to get outside fast and grab an eagerly waiting Pluto.

"It sure doesn't seem like Christmas Day inside your house," Sam commented. Actually, Sam thought with a sigh, Avi's home did have the same warm holiday feeling of the Goodman house in previous years, but that wasn't what he was getting at. "Doesn't it seem weird to be celebrating Hanukkah when everywhere you turn it's all about Christmas?"

"Weird?" Avi repeated. "No, it's too much fun. But it is

easier to feel like you're part of all the holiday stuff when Hanukkah falls around the same time as Christmas," he added, pulling his stocking cap out of his pocket.

"Otherwise?"

Avi shrugged. "It's harder. It's Christmas all around you whether you're celebrating it or not. But like my parents always say, it's not our holiday."

Today Christmas didn't feel much like Sam's holiday, either. To change the subject, he asked casually, "So are you going to the New Year's Eve dance?"

Avi didn't hesitate. "Sure."

"I told my family I was going, and of course my mother was all excited about a dance, so I guess I'll go, too." Sam pulled Pluto away from a garbage can that seemed to hold all sorts of tempting surprises.

"I think it'll be good," Avi said. Avi was an optimist. Sometimes Sam couldn't stand that about Avi.

"What'll be so good about it?" Sam asked. "We have to get dressed up, and then we have to ask girls to dance."

"They might ask us," Avi pointed out.

Again with the optimism, Sam thought. "There's only one girl I want to dance with, anyway."

Avi groaned. "Not Heather."

"We had a good time together at the mall," Sam argued. Well, *he* had, anyway.

"Fine, whatever," Avi said. "As long as you go."

"You sound pretty excited about it," Sam commented.

That was Avi's cue to try to appear laid back. "Yeah. Well, why not? I have to get some dancing practice in, anyway. There's going to be a band at my bar mitzvah."

"Are you inviting Heather?" Sam wanted to know.

Avi nodded reluctantly. "Mom said I have to invite everyone in our homeroom, so yeah, I'm inviting Heather."

Avi's bar mitzvah was starting to have some potential. "When is it, again?" Sam asked.

"The middle of March. Not that far away," Avi said with a touch more worry than anticipation in his voice.

They had just gotten to the park, when Jeremy Marcos appeared, walking his dog, Buster. Sam felt the name was an attempt to add a masculine luster to a yappy little terrier that was clearly a wimp. Buster and Pluto sniffed at each other cautiously.

Jeremy pulled his dog back. "Come here Buster. Stay away from that Goodman mutt. What's his name again, Sam? Some planet? Ur-*anus*?"

"Ha, ha. You know it's Pluto." Sam scowled at Avi, who was laughing for real.

"So what did you get for Christmas?" Jeremy demanded.

Sam rattled off the games and clothes he had gotten. He didn't mention the key chain.

Avi explained that he only received one present for each night of Hanukkah. Last night's had been a Cubs sweatshirt.

"So you get one present a night, and there's eight nights?" Jeremy was no math genius, but even he could add that up. "Well, that's okay, that's probably about what you'd get on Christmas morning, anyway."

Sam asked about Jeremy's gifts. "I got a bike. Mountain bike. That was the best. Clothes, CDs, a book" — Jeremy made a face — "from my grandmother."

"No video games?" Sam asked impatiently. The wind was starting to blow, it was getting cold, and he wanted to hear what, if anything, Heather had said about him.

The light dawned. "Oh yeah, last night, Buried Treasure. From Heather. It's pretty good."

"I thought it would be."

"Well, I guess I'm glad that you helped Heather pick something. She probably would have gotten me a fake dog doo on her own."

That would have worked, Sam thought. He tried to come up with another way to bring Heather's name into the conversation. What had she and Jeremy done last evening? Did they have fun? And once and for all had she mentioned his name? Nothing occurred to Sam, however, that could be said without him sounding like a complete and utter sap. He mentally high-fived himself for at least being smart enough to know that.

"We were just talking about the New Year's dance," Avi said. "Are you going?"

"I'm there," Jeremy said. "What about you two?"

Sam had a brief vision of floating on the dance floor with Heather in his arms. "Me too," he said, suddenly catching a little of Avi's optimism. "I think it will be fun."

After saying good-bye to Jeremy and Avi, Sam took one more turn around the block so Pluto would be good and tired by the time he got home. Still feeling good about the upcoming dance, he told himself that now that Christmas was almost behind him, things would get back to normal.

"The stupid holiday stuff is over," Sam informed Pluto, who seemed glad to hear it. "The only holiday I'm going to think about now is New Year's Eve. I'm going to a dance," he said, letting himself feel excited. "Heather Daniels is going to be there. She knows who I am now."

Pluto turned and looked at him balefully.

"No, really," Sam assured his dog. "It's going to be fun."

CHAPTER EIGHT

What had he gotten himself into? When Sam had boldly declared to Jeremy and Avi (and Pluto) that the New Year's dance was going to be fun, he clearly hadn't known what he was talking about. If the dance itself was anything like the prep work, he was looking at one of the most miserable evenings of his life.

The misery had started at the Christmas Day lunch. It seemed odd to Sam to be going to a restaurant called Seaside when they were a couple of thousand miles from the nearest sea. But even if the restaurant had been called The Chicago River, going out to eat on Christmas felt strange and formal. Usually, his mother made a turkey, and everyone helped prepare the dinner — Sam's specialty was smashing the potatoes — while the Goodmans' ample CD collection of Christmas carols, blaring in the background, provided the soundtrack for the festivities.

But today, the Goodmans trooped listlessly into the Seaside, uncomfortably dressed, the females in high heels, the males tugging at their ties, and halfhearted smiles all around. As Sam scanned the menu handed to him by the waiter, he was displeased to find that turkey wasn't even on the menu.

"I thought there would be turkey," Mrs. Goodman murmured, looking upset.

"It's better this way," Mr. Goodman said, trying to rally. "It would only be a pale imitation of yours."

"But what am I supposed to eat?" Maxie asked with a slight whine in his voice.

Good question, thought Sam as he looked over the menu again. Halibut, yes, salmon, something called grouper — there were lots of fish dishes. Sam hated fish, which he considered slimy and smelly, so he opted for one of the pasta dishes. Linguini didn't exactly shout Christmas dinner, but he supposed it fit right in with the way things were going.

Sitting in the festively decorated restaurant, waiting for food no one really wanted, the Goodmans were on their best behavior, which translated into no talk about Christmas Eve, grandmothers, or religion. That was fine with Sam, but it meant that everyone just sort of nibbled around the edges of conversations, like they were nibbling at their food. Mrs. Goodman talked a little about her fourth graders, and Mr. Goodman mentioned that he had a big case coming up, but the tax law that he practiced was so boring, no one asked him any questions about it, not even Mrs. Goodman, who usually tried to appear interested. But as dinner was served, a subject came up that they could all discuss with hearty abandon. Unfortunately, it was the New Year's Eve dance.

At first, the topic of New Year's Eve doings had been directed at Ellen.

"A get-together with friends," she had responded curtly to her father's inquiry of what she "had going" on December 31.

"Which friends?" Mrs. Goodman asked.

"I don't know yet."

"Where will you be?" Mr. Goodman asked.

"I'm not sure." Ellen clamped her mouth shut, silently chewing her swordfish.

Mrs. Goodman, knowing a dead end when she heard one, looked elsewhere for news of New Year's. "Well, I know someone's plans." She beamed at Sam, seeming truly happy for the first time in days.

Sam's eyes darted involuntarily toward the exit.

Ellen put down her fork. "That's right, Sam has that big dance on New Year's Eve. Tell us about it, Sam."

Trying to muster some dignity, Sam replied, "I haven't actually decided whether I'm going or not." This statement, of course, wasn't technically true, especially since it was only mere hours ago that he had been telling everyone from his friends to his dog that he was practically counting the days until the dance. Still, he hoped his answer might forestall further comments. This was not to be.

"But you told the grandmas you were going," Maxie pointed out.

"Of course, you're going," Mr. Goodman said.

"It's your first dance. It's *always* good to try something new," his mother added.

Those particular words stirred memories in Sam. Hadn't that been the same phrase and intonation his mother had used when she first sent him off to playgroup? And to Cub Scouts? Both experiences, he seemed to recall, had ended in tears, with him vowing never to try anything new again. Sam stared up at the ceiling. Conceding to himself that his supposed indecision about the dance wasn't enough to stop the conversation, Sam nevertheless hoped that talk would soon enough turn to something else. But no, the subject was launched.

Who would be there? Which parents were going to chaperone? What kind of music would be played? Was there a dress code? When would it begin? When would it end?

Despite minimal input from Sam, who declined to give out even what information he knew, the rest of the family was able to keep the subject of the dance going until it was time to order dessert. Then, mercifully, Maxie, himself bored with Sam's dance, changed topics to a discussion of his own New Year's Eve plans with his babysitter.

"I'm thinking taffy apples," Maxie informed his family. "They're fun to make. And I want to rent some of those Freddy movies. I'll watch them till midnight."

"Who's Freddy?" Mr. Goodman asked. "I used to read a series of books about a pig named Freddy. Did they turn those into movies?"

Everyone just looked at Mr. Goodman. The rest of the luncheon was taken up with Mrs. Goodman — and Mr. Goodman, once he understood who Freddy Krueger was — explaining to Maxie that they didn't want him watching movies that would give him bad dreams, that midnight was too late for growing boys, and that taffy apples were bad for his teeth.

"Don't worry," Ellen comforted him. "Someday you'll be old enough to do whatever you want. However, when that day comes, you won't want to make taffy apples."

With so much attention having been lavished on the dance at Christmas lunch, Sam assumed the subject was closed indefinitely. How wrong he was. The very next day, Mrs. Goodman said to Sam, "When would you like to go shopping for a sports coat?"

"A sports coat?" Sam exclaimed. "What do I need that for?"

His mother looked at him quizzically. "The dance, of course."

"I told you, I don't know what anyone's wearing to the dance," Sam said, trying to stall.

Talking as much to herself as to Sam, Mrs. Goodman said, "True, maybe slacks and a sweater are more appropriate. But you'll need a sports coat for Avi's bar mitzvah. And there will be others. . . ." She refocused her eyes on Sam. "I'll make some calls."

Sam decided to head over to the alcove off the family room, where the computer was located, to see who was online, while his mother got on the telephone, though who one called about sports coats, he had no idea.

Avi was online, and so was Jeremy, so Sam decided to ask about the dress code for the dance.

SAM: Nyeve? What are you wearing?

AVI: pants

JEREMY: nothing

"So funny I forgot to laugh," Sam was about to write, but just then he noticed Maxie waiting patiently in the doorway, looking as if he wanted to talk. Turning away from the screen, he gestured his brother to come closer. "What's up, Max?"

"We forgot to light the Hanukkah candles last night," Maxie informed him.

"I guess we did." The family had gone to a movie after Christmas lunch, and then everyone had gone their separate ways. Ellen, out with friends, and his parents to visit with some neighbors down the street. Sam had flirted with the idea of going to Avi's Hanukkah party, but he'd had enough "festivities" for the day and was content to stay home. So he had read the book he needed to finish for school, while Maxie was downstairs watching television. "Did you remember?" Sam asked.

Maxie nodded.

"So why didn't you tell me? You and I could have lit the candles."

"It seemed too sad. We were all supposed to light them together." Maxie turned away.

"Come here, buddy." He reached out and gave Maxie a small hug. "I'll tell Mom and Dad, and we'll be sure to light them tonight."

"Whatever," Maxie said with a shrug.

Sam hated, just hated, to hear that. Little kids should not be going around saying "whatever." It was fine when you were twelve and knew that life could break your heart, yet you were ready to soldier on and pretend not to care. But someone Maxie's age should not be trying to hide the sad stuff under a "whatever."

"I'll fix it," Sam promised.

"Okay," Maxie said more cheerfully. It made Sam feel both good and nervous to know his little brother had such confidence in him.

Sam waited till Maxie went next door to a friend's house. Then he marched down to the basement, where his parents were cleaning. That had been one of his dad's Christmas (or Hanukkah) presents to his mother. Mr. Goodman had given her a card saying he would clean out the basement, something his wife had been asking him to do for about as long as Sam could remember.

The dank basement was full of Goodman family history. One side of the room had a bunch of old furniture that Sam remembered from their former house, the one they had moved from when Sam was five. There were a few kitchen chairs and a couple of lamps that Mrs. Goodman kept saying she was going to find a place for, their shades now colored gray from dust. A beat-up dresser was filled with his mother's unfinished knitting projects, mostly baby sweaters for children who were now teenagers. Stuck in a corner was a card table that was stacked with boxes of books that were still waiting to be unpacked from their move seven years ago.

The motley display of relics, surprisingly, was the most interesting part of the crowded basement. Everything else was a hodgepodge. Next to the washer and dryer, clothes were hanging from a freestanding rack, and beside the appliances were bulging metal file cabinets that held the gamut from old tax returns to travel brochures for vacations the Goodmans would never take. A half-empty bag of charcoal sat next to several half-empty bags of mulch and fertilizer and other gardening equipment. Cardboard boxes were scattered across the basement floor like an obstacle course, and it was a toss-up whether it was harder to make one's way around them or navigate the laundry baskets that also littered the dark landscape.

Sam gingerly approached his parents, who were standing under a single burning bulb, going through a small carton of photographs.

"I've got to get these into albums," Mrs. Goodman said, holding one up to the light. "Oh, I think this is one of you as a baby." She passed it over to her husband.

Mr. Goodman chuckled. "Look at those curls. I was sweet."

Mrs. Goodman leaned her head in for another look. "And those big brown eyes, just like Ellen's."

His parents seemed relaxed with each other. Sam hated to interrupt, but he had promised Maxie.

"Mom, Dad —"

"Oh, come here, Sam," his father said, waving the picture at him. "Look at me when I was about a year old."

Sam dutifully looked at the photo his dad held out to him, "Cute, but Dad —"

"I should really put together an album that's just baby pictures, all of us," his mother said, taking the picture back.

"Mom —"

"Are you ready to go shopping, Sam? I was talking to Avi's mother. I think I'll buy you a sports coat and a new sweater. The after-Christmas sales have started. . . ."

"Maxie is all upset because we forgot to light the Hanukkah candles." There.

Mr. Goodman swore. Not a very bad word, but Sam was surprised, anyway, because he always watched his language around the kids. "Can't we even get it together to light those candles for more than one day?"

"We?" Mrs. Goodman repeated, her voice now cold. "You said *you'd* take care of Hanukkah."

"Excuse me, Annie," Mr. Goodman's voice was equally frosty. "I wasn't implying it was your fault."

"Well, I should hope not," his mother answered, giving no ground. "Hanukkah is *your* holiday."

"I thought we agreed it was everyone's holiday this year."

"Hey," Sam interrupted. "I didn't tell you so you'd start fighting."

Both of his parents looked at him as if they'd forgotten he was there.

"No, of course not, Sam," his mother said, in a somewhat warmer tone. "You were right to tell us."

"Yes, we'll take care of it," his father added.

Sam looked at them doubtfully.

"I suppose we should get some small presents to open up tonight when we light the candles," Mr. Goodman said carefully as he tossed his baby picture back in the box.

"Yes, that's a good idea," Mrs. Goodman agreed. "I'll pick them up."

"You don't have to," Mr. Goodman said.

"No, I wanted to go shopping with Sam, anyway. I'll get something. Sam, why don't you get ready, and we'll go to the mall."

That sounded like fun, Sam thought grimly. But he stomped upstairs, listening for the sound of raised voices from the basement all the way to the living room.

Like his father, his mother used rides in the car to peer into Sam's psyche. Had one of them gotten the idea first, and passed it to the other, Sam wondered, or had it sprung from each of them full-blown? Mrs. Goodman didn't deal with big issues in the car, however. She just talked about what he and his friends were doing, how school was going, drawing him out before he realized he was revealing too much. Today, though, she was uncharacteristically quiet. Perhaps it was his turn to steer the conversation.

"Mom, I don't like the way this whole Christmas/ Hanukkah thing is putting everyone in a bad mood."

"I don't like it, either, Sam," his mother agreed.

"Let's just do the Hanukkah thing, get it over with, and go back to normal."

Mrs. Goodman turned toward the mall. "I don't know if we can, Sam."

"Why not?" Sam asked with surprise.

"We can't just shove this religion thing under the rug anymore. When your father and I got married, we decided we weren't going to raise you children in any particular religion, and would let you choose what you wanted to be when you got older."

"That sounds okay," Sam said.

"But it makes me sad. I loved going to church when I was your age. I feel like you're missing something."

"I don't," Sam said promptly.

"That's because you don't know what you're missing. And your father, for all his ambivalent feelings about religion, would like you to know more about Judaism. He even mentioned Maxie going to Hebrew school."

"So he can be bar mitzvahed?" Sam asked with surprise.

His mother nodded. "Eventually."

"Did he want me to go to Hebrew school?"

"It never came up when you were Maxie's age."

That made Sam feel odd. Why did his father want Maxie to be Jewish, and hadn't cared whether he was? "So I guess you don't want him to go, to Hebrew school," Sam phrased the question carefully.

"I don't know what I want, Sam," Mrs. Goodman said in a troubled voice. "As you got older I thought that I just wanted you kids to have some religion, no matter what it is. But if I'm honest, maybe I wanted it to be mine."

"Why does there have to be so much fighting about religion?" Sam burst out. "By the way, I asked God. He didn't answer."

Mrs. Goodman gave Sam a soft smile. "Maybe He just hasn't answered *yet*."

"I talked to Ellen, too. She said it's about people thinking they have to be right and making other people wrong. But if everybody worships the same God, they should all believe the same thing."

"They do, in a way," Mrs. Goodman said as she pulled into a parking space. "All religions teach if people are good to one another, are charitable, and try to be the best they can be, the world becomes a better place."

"Well, it doesn't seem like that's what's happening," Sam grumbled.

"It happens one person at a time," his mother said, turning off the car. "One person at a time."

Sam was so tired of thinking about religion that shopping for clothes suddenly felt like a pleasant change. At least, that's what he thought until he started trying them on. Shopping always made his mother feel better no matter what was going on, and this particular expedition seemed particularly to perk her up. The mall was as busy as it had been before Christmas. The same presents that had been so lovingly taken out of the stores were now being hauled back by dissatisfied recipients. The good news, as far as Mrs. Goodman was concerned, anyway, was that everything in the mall was on sale.

This fact did not speed the process; rather, it seemed to slow it down. Not only did Sam have to try on every jacket that might look good on him, his mother also wanted to find the best bargain. So they fought the crowds from one end of the mall to the other, until Sam finally had to put his foot down.

"No more!"

"But, Sam —"

"Please. I'll take the blue one at Lord & Taylor, or that brown one at the Gap, but I don't want to try on one more jacket. I can't."

Mrs. Goodman had to pull Sam into a shoe store doorway so they wouldn't get trampled. "All right," Mrs. Goodman conceded. "The blue one. But then we have to pick out a shirt and tie, and maybe some new slacks."

"Mom! You can pick those out. Whatever you want."

"I guess I can do that. But Sam, don't forget you have to go to the barber before the dance. There's one here at the mall —"

"No!"

"Can you go tomorrow?"

Would this never end? Sam wondered. He was surprised his mother didn't want him to have his teeth cleaned before New Year's.

"Fine, the barber. Tomorrow. But for now I'm done. Where should I meet you and when?"

Mrs. Goodman looked at her watch. "I shouldn't be long. I'll just get everything at Lord & Taylor. Meet me at McDonald's in half an hour."

Sam felt like he could fly through the mall, so relieved he was to be free of shopping and, yes, his mother. He debated going to the food court right now to see if any of his friends were there, but decided he just wanted to enjoy the feeling of being alone. Maybe he would head over to the bookstore to check out the new sports magazines. Or maybe he would go to the small arcade tucked away on the main level. The games there were mostly dumb, plenty of golf and stock car racing and nothing too violent, but Sam had to admit he still liked the noise and color that came with any arcade.

Riding the escalator down to the main level, Sam felt like he was one of those Greek gods surveying things from Mount Olympus. People were dashing here and there, as if their tasks were the most important things in the world, when half of them were probably just returning bad-looking clothes and too-big underwear. What had happened to those Greek gods, anyway? Sam wondered. Plenty of people had believed in them, back in the day. Did they just fade away once better gods came along, or had they never really existed at all? Hey God, Sam said silently, maybe next time I'll ask Jupiter my questions instead of You. Probably no one has asked him anything for the last couple thousand years. Maybe he has time to answer me. Sam thought he heard God laugh, but realized the hearty sound came from a bearded senior citizen in the midst of conversation, going up on the adjoining escalator. The man caught his eye, but Sam turned away.

After walking as briskly as possible through the post-holiday throng, Sam finally reached the arcade. It was packed with kids, and Sam figured there was no point in staying in the crowded room for even a minute, but as he turned to leave, he caught sight of a familiar mane of blond hair, almost hidden in a corner. Heather!

A part of him wanted to turn tail and head for McDonald's, but after hours of boring shopping and being the obedient son, another part wanted to do something bold and exciting. So before he could let himself think too much, he walked right over to Heather and said, "Hi."

"Hi," she replied, looking slightly surprised to see him appear so suddenly. "Are you here to . . ." She gestured to the yelling kids crashing away on the machines.

"Oh, no," Sam said with what he hoped was a hearty laugh. "I was just walking by and saw you standing here."

"I'm supposed to be watching my sister." Heather pointed to a girl about nine who looked like a mini-Heather, steering manically around a stock car track.

"She got better?"

"Oh, yes. Lucy was sick just long enough to wreck our plans."

Sam tried to think of something else to say since Heather wasn't putting forth much conversational effort. "Done anything fun over vacation?"

"I just told you, we didn't get to go away," she replied bitterly.

"But, maybe —"

"And most of my friends are on vacation. There's no one around worth hanging out with."

Sam knew there were plenty of seventh-grade girls around. He had seen some of them at the mall. As the silence thickened, Sam wondered if he should suggest a few names of girls Heather might call. No, he didn't have the nerve for that. Heather looked so miserable, though, he wished he could come up with something to make her feel better.

Suddenly, out of his mouth came the words, "Are you going to the New Year's Eve dance at the community center?"

Heather blinked. "Are you?" she parried.

Sam would have liked to have heard Heather's answer first, but he was stuck, stuck to the tune of a new jacket, pants, and shirt, and there was no use denying that he wasn't. "Yeah, I'm going."

"I might, depending on who else will be there," Heather allowed.

Hey, Sam wanted to say, I just told you *I'll* be there, but that seemed even more gutsy than suggesting potential friends. Instead, he said, "It might be fun."

Heather cocked her head and looked at him as if she were seeing Sam for the first time. "Yeah, I guess it might."

Lucy, looking pink-cheeked and not the least bit ill, ran up and tugged on Heather's arm. "I'm bored."

Sam was afraid that Heather might say, "I'm bored, too," but instead, after grabbing her packages, she gave Sam a slight smile and said, "So maybe I'll see you at the dance."

Sam watched Heather and Lucy disappear into the crowd. "I'll be there," he murmured.

CHAPTER NINE

"You look adorable!" Mrs. Goodman bubbled.

"Like a little doll," Ellen added sarcastically.

Sam stood in front of his family feeling like he was clothed as much in embarrassment as he was in chinos, a turtleneck sweater, and a new jacket.

His father seemed to sense his discomfort. "All right," Mr. Goodman said, "let's just take the pictures so Sam can get to the dance."

But Sam, decked out in his party finery, and a camera in his mother's hand proved a deadly combination. How many photos did she need — or even want — of him dressed up? The answer seemed to be plenty. After several pictures by himself, in front of the fireplace, he posed with Ellen and Maxie, who had been called into the living room. Ellen smiled at the camera, Sam scowled, Maxie appeared bewildered at the fuss. Then his mother handed Ellen the camera so she could take several snaps of Sam with his parents.

"Everyone say 'life of the party'," she directed wickedly.

Sam disentangled himself from his parents. "I'm surprised you don't want one of me and Pluto," he muttered.

Mrs. Goodman took back the camera. "Good idea. But don't get too close to him. I don't want Pluto getting any hair on your new jacket."

After a groaning Sam had finished posing with a very uncooperative Pluto, he got up and said, "I'm going to be late."

"You're right," his mother said, surprised, as if she had nothing to do with holding up his departure.

"Okay, let's go," Ellen said, heading toward the closet. His parents, who finally seemed in a good mood, had to get ready for their own evening out, so Ellen, who was leaving much later for her New Year's gathering with friends, had been designated to drive him to the dance.

This was better, in some ways. Sam didn't think he could face the drive with his father. What if he chose the ride as a good time for yet another sex talk? His mother would be better, but she'd fuss at him. Tell him to comb his hair or remind him to say hello to the chaperones, something probably no one had done since the dinosaurs were dancing. She would make him even more nervous than he already was.

But going with Ellen had its own downside. This was a perfect opportunity for her to tease him. She had already taken to calling him the Heartthrob of Hamilton Junior High, and the seventh-grade Chick Magnet. So it was with some trepidation that Sam slid into the car alongside his sister.

To his surprise as she drove the short distance to the Community House, Ellen was quiet, her irrepressible sarcasm for once under wraps. Feeling a little uncomfortable, Sam asked her if everything was all right.

"Huh? Oh sure."

"Who's going to be at your party tonight?" Sam said to make conversation.

"A bunch of kids from high school. I've seen most of them over vacation, but there's a few who were away, so getting together should be fun."

They didn't say anything else until Ellen parked in front of the Community House. Then she turned to him. "Sam, do me a favor."

"What?"

"Dance with a fat girl."

Sam was taken aback. There were a couple of fat girls in his class, but Sam didn't want to dance with them. "Why should I do that?"

Ellen stared out the windshield. "Nobody ever dances with the fat girls. It would be a nice thing to do."

Sure, it would be, Sam thought. For someone else. But Ellen was looking at him expectantly. He had to say something. "Well, maybe I will. Sure, I'll think about it."

His sister seemed satisfied. At least she didn't say anything else, except "Have fun" as he got out of the car.

As he made his way up the stairs, Sam wondered where Ellen's request had come from. He thought back to when she was in junior high. He was just a little kid, but he remembered her as being pretty chubby. Even now, she was always worrying about her weight, though she looked fine to him. Had she gone to a dance and stood by herself all night? Sam didn't like to think about Ellen hanging around, waiting — hoping — for someone to choose her as a partner. She was so great — funny, smart — even if she was his sister. The thought of her standing alone made him feel sad.

After handing his coat to a parent, Sam walked into the auditorium-size room that took up most of the community center. The building itself was old and was used for functions like small concerts and lectures. There had even been a baseball memorabilia show right here in this very room. But tonight the space looked completely different. The almost circular room with the small stage opposite the entrance was decorated within an inch of its life. Sparkly streamers were hanging from the ceiling, and right in the middle of those twisted garlands was a disco ball covered with small mirrors that reflected light as it turned in the air. Scattered tables along the walls were covered with linen tablecloths on which some parent, no doubt, had sprinkled tiny iridescent stars. All this glitter was a little too much for Sam. He wished he could put on sunglasses. Not only would it cut the glare, it might look very cool — and give him more confidence to walk in the room.

As it was, Sam just stood in the entrance, gazing around, trying to get his bearings. There were seventh and eighth graders from the two junior highs in Evanston, so he didn't know all of the kids milling about. But it was easy to pick out the kids from his school since they were standing together in clumps. He spotted his friends, Avi, Jeremy, and a couple of the other boys he hung out with, holding up the wall on one side of the room, laughing and joking around with one another. Closer to the action were the eighth-grade boys. Sam looked at them with narrowed eyes. Only one grade older, but they seemed decades more confident. Sam watched as one boy, Robert Erlich, sauntered over and asked a pretty girl with red hair to dance. All he had to do was hold out his hand, and the girl seemed to melt into him. How did someone only a year older pull off that move?

One circle of girls stood near the stage, where the DJ, wearing a vest as flashy as the streamers, was adjusting his equipment. But Sam's eyes quickly shifted from the DJ to the girls, because in the middle of the group stood a laughing Heather Daniels. She had come after all.

Sam felt as if he were in one of those sappy movies his mother and sister liked, where the hero and heroine stare into each other's eyes, and — ba bing! — it's as if everyone else in the room fades away. The only difference between that movie moment and this one was that Heather wasn't looking at him. Okay, so that was a big difference, but this was almost as good, because, Sam consoled himself, it gave him more time to look at Heather. She was wearing a dress that was red, short, shiny, and sleeveless. Wasn't she freezing? Sam wondered. He had never seen Heather wear her hair any way but falling around her shoulders. Tonight, however, it was pulled back, and the style showed off her pretty face. Sam wasn't sure if it was the dress or the hairdo, or maybe the touch of lipstick she seemed to be wearing, but she looked almost as old as Ellen.

Without another glance, he turned on his heel and moved quickly toward his friends, his heart sinking. Heather looked as though she could be a model in *CosmoGIRL!* Sam caught a glimpse of himself as he walked by one of the room's glass patio doors, and he stopped for a couple seconds, using the glass as a mirror. His outfit was okay, but he still felt like a boy dressed up in his father's clothes. Heather wouldn't have a minute for him. And why should she? It was so clear she could do better.

"Hey, Goodman," called Will Jackson from a few feet away. "What's happenin'?"

Sam put on his game face and went over to his friends. "You tell me," Sam said, slapping Will's hand. "Is this party any good?"

"Not yet," Avi said glumly. "We haven't danced or anything, if that's what you mean."

"Why not?" Sam responded.

Jeremy gestured over to the clutch of seventh-grade girls. "They're all just standing around. Over there."

"So are you guys. Over here," Sam noted.

"Okay," Ben O'Meara said. "You ask somebody to dance. Get things going."

Sam felt caught. He didn't want to be the one to start the dancing, but if someone didn't have the guts to do it, this was going to be a very long night.

The DJ's voice coming over the speakers interrupted Sam's thoughts. "The next one is ladies' choice. Girls, go get your guys."

This was a break. Let the girls put themselves on the line. Sam and his friends looked at one another nervously. Would anyone come over to their particular huddle and ask for a dance? To Sam's surprise, some of the girls were heading in their direction. Sam kept his head down until he felt a tap on his shoulder. He looked up and there was Vicki Freeman, frowning. "Want to dance?"

Sam had known Vicki since their mothers had taken them as toddlers to a mom-and-tot group called Babies on Board, and both families had the photographs to prove it. Sam had the sneaking suspicion that someday he'd be as embarrassed by the pictures his mom had taken today as he was by the photos of Vicki and him practically naked jumping around in a wading pool.

"What's wrong?" Sam asked as an unenthusiastic Vicki pulled him out onto the dance floor. "You don't look too excited to be dancing with me."

"I don't want to dance with you. I want to dance with Avi."

"So why didn't you ask him?" Sam asked, as he started dancing with Vicki, anyway.

"It was easier to ask you," Vicki said flatly.

Sam could understand that. Asking Vicki to dance would have been a lot easier than asking Heather. And it was much easier to put his arm around her waist for a slow dance. "So, do you want me to tell Avi to ask you to dance?"

Vicki's freckled face turned pink. "Would you?"

Sam shrugged. "Sure."

"What if he doesn't want to?"

Sam knew Avi well enough to know that he'd be so flattered that anyone wanted to dance with him, he'd happily ask the girl, whoever she was. But sharing that particular bit of information might hurt Vicki's feelings. "Oh, I think he will," was all Sam said.

The song ended, and another slow song began. Since they were in the middle of the room anyway, Vicki said, "You want to just keep dancing?" Maybe she was thinking of dancing with Avi, but Vicki closed her eyes and didn't seem to want to talk to him anymore. That gave Sam the chance to look around the dance floor. The slow music wafting through the room had drawn several of the couples closer together. Some of the eighth graders were dancing so close, you couldn't see a speck of light between them. The girls had their heads down on the boys' shoulders, the boys' hands were draped casually around the small of the girls' backs. One or two of the bolder guys seemed to be letting their hands drift even farther south. Where did they get the nerve? Sam couldn't conceive of trying that move on Heather.

Where *was* Heather? Sam wondered as he glanced around the dance floor. There. It was pretty easy to spot her in that red dress, even if she was all the way across the room. She was dancing with Hank Chin, one of the brightest kids in the eighth grade. Just to torture himself, Sam decided to get a closer look. Even though Sam was almost as tall as Hank, he felt about as big as a second grader as he maneuvered an un-suspecting Vicki nearer to the targeted couple.

It took a minute or two to push/pull himself and Vicki into the right position. Sam studied Heather over Vicki's shoulder. She certainly wasn't leaning into Hank the way some of the other girls on the dance floor were with their partners. If anything, the look on her faced spelled b-o-r-e-d. Just as Sam was about to avert his eyes, Heather glanced in his direction. He wondered if his face was getting as red as Vicki's had when she'd brought up dancing with Avi. Thoughts suddenly started flitting through his brain like lightning bugs powering up on a summer night. Turn away, one commanded; no, smile at her; no, wait, talk to Vicki. No, make a joke, and Vicki will laugh uproariously, and Heather will think you're a great wit. . . .

Before Sam could do any of those things, Heather focused in on him, and silently mouthed two words: Help Me.

No, thought Sam, shot with confusion. I've got that wrong. *Help me?* Why would Heather say that? To him? But she did say something, unless she was just pretending to be a fish gasping for air. And why would she do *that?*

Out of the corner of his eye, Sam saw that now Hank was facing him, not Heather. He looked as happy as Sam would be to be dancing with Heather. Sam silently tried to form words that might sound like Help Me. Elf meal? Elm tree?

"What did you say?" Vicki asked, jerking back and looking at Sam.

"I didn't say anything," he replied defensively.

"Yes, you did. You were, like, whispering 'elm tree' or something."

Luckily for Sam, the music ended at that moment. His laugh was stiff and small. "I don't think so, Freeman."

Vicki didn't look as if she was buying it, but she had something else she wanted to say as Sam escorted her back to where her friends were standing, just as he had been told to do by his mother. "So, about Avi, um, you won't forget?"

Actually, he had almost forgotten already, but he just nodded and said, "Sure, I'll take care of it."

Sam made his way back to where he had left the guys. The ice seemed to be broken, because more dancers were crowding the floor. He walked by Jeremy, who was moving to the music with a girl Sam didn't know. Will was dancing, too. But Avi was still where Sam had left him.

"Didn't anyone ask you for the ladies' choice?" Sam asked him.

Avi shook his head.

"Well, good news. Vicki was too nervous to ask you. I was second choice."

"No way." Avi looked decidedly perkier than he had a second ago.

"Yeah, way. Go ask her to dance."

Avi shook his head.

"What?" Sam said. "Why not?"

"I will. Not just yet. I want to wait for another slow dance," Avi added shyly.

As long as Avi was going to stay around for a few minutes, Sam decided to pick his brain. "Say, Avi, what do you think I'm saying." He mouthed the words "help me."

Avi looked at Sam quizzically. "Is this some kind of a joke?"

"No, really, what do you think I'm saying?" he insisted, before silently repeating "help me."

Avi tried. "Hell meat?" he guessed.

Sam took this as encouragement. Hell meat was pretty close.

"What's this all about?" Avi demanded.

"I think Heather whispered 'help me' when she danced by me with Hank Chin."

Avi looked at Sam like he was nuts. "Why would she do that?"

That's what Sam asked himself for the next half hour. He jostled with a bunch of kids at the punch and cookie table as he grabbed some food, and he asked another girl in his class to dance, a fast one this time. But all the time he was trying to figure out if he had seen what he thought he saw and, if so, what he should have done about it.

As Sam's dance ended, he looked around to see Heather's whereabouts. Another slow dance had just started, and the lights had been lowered enough so that the disco ball was shooting twinkling lights all over the room. Some of the sparkling bits of illuminations were showered around Heather, who was once again circling the room with Hank.

Sam willed Heather to look in his direction, but she didn't. Then the voice of the DJ boomed out over the music. "Guys, this is your chance to cut in. Just tap some other guy on the shoulder and start dancing with his girl." Sam froze. The DJ's order seemed as if it were directed right at him. Before he had time to change his mind, Sam walked determinedly up to Heather and Hank, stuck out his hand, and tapped his forefinger on Hank's shoulder.

Hank turned around and gave Sam a slight grin. "Go ahead. I figured I wouldn't be able to get through this dance after that DJ opened his big mouth." He handed Heather over to Sam.

Now that he had her, Sam wasn't quite sure what to do with her. Heather looked as bored now swaying with him as she had with Hank. Since he had a steam of courage up, Sam decided he might as well say what was on his mind. "Uh, Heather?"

"Hmmm?"

"Did you say something to me earlier? When you were dancing with Hank. Well, not exactly say something —"

Heather finally smiled. "Oh, you picked up on that?"

"It sounded, well, looked like you said —"

"Help me." Heather finished for him.

"Yeah," Sam said with relief. At least he hadn't been hallucinating.

"You must have thought I was crazy," Heather giggled.

"I just wondered what was up," Sam replied.

"I'm tired of dancing," Heather announced. She turned and walked over to the side of the room where there were some empty chairs, as a regretful Sam trailed behind her. He had been so fixated on getting the "help me" thing straightened out, he hadn't had time to enjoy his hand around Heather's waist, hers on his shoulder. When they were settled, she continued, "I needed to be rescued."

"And you picked me?" As soon as the words were out of his mouth, Sam realized that didn't sound cool, not cool at all, but Heather didn't seem to notice. Smoothing back her hair and readjusting her ponytail, Heather responded, "Well, you were there and you helped me at the mall . . . I don't know, it just came out." Finished with her hair, she turned to Sam and smiled. "You didn't mind, did you?"

Sam looked down, looked up, and shrugged. "No. Anyway, why did you want to get away from Hank?"

Heather looked at him for a second or two, then turned her attention to the dance floor. "He's just not my type." She frowned. "I was trying to make that clear when he asked me to dance."

The nerve? That seemed an odd way to put it. The silence that followed began to border on the uncomfortable. "Want to dance again?" Sam asked hopefully.

Heather shook her head no. She looked down at the slim red watch on her wrist. "Can't. I need to get going. My dad's picking me up soon."

"Now?" Sam protested. "It's early. Everything's just getting started."

"I know," Heather replied; there was that rosebud pout again. "But my parents are having a big New Year's Eve thing tonight, and they want me on display. They said I could come here for a little while if I spent most of the night at home."

Heather stood, and Sam popped up like a jack-in-the-box. "Do you want me to wait outside with you or something?"

Heather smiled, and this time it looked more real than the other times he had seen her smile. "That's okay. My dad's probably out there already. But thanks, really. For everything."

Sam didn't know how long he stood there after Heather left. As soon as he realized he was standing, he sat back down on the hard folding chair, watching the wavelike motion of the dancers without really seeing them. After a while, one person standing near the refreshment table caught his eye. It was Elizabeth Browne, one of the fat girls in his class. Not gigantic, maybe, but more than chubby. She was nice, though. They had worked on a science project last year. Elizabeth looked lonely standing there by herself, with an expression on her face that was a mix of nervousness and hope. Sam thought about what Ellen had said in the car, and he knew this would be a perfect opportunity to honor his sister's request. This particular slow dance was half over, anyway, and Heather was gone, so she wouldn't see him with Elizabeth and wonder why he was dancing with her. But Sam didn't get up; he didn't want to. You've got the rest of your life to dance with a fat girl, he told himself. So he leaned back and did what he really wanted to do: sit on a metal chair, stare into space, and think about Heather.

CHAPTER TEN

Heather was tickling the soles of his feet, running her fingers up and down, up and down. It made him want to laugh. And she was calling his name, "Sammy. Hey, Sammy."

Sam opened one sleepy eye. There were only two people who called him Sammy, and neither one was Heather. He was sure Grandma Sally wasn't tickling his feet. Pulling the covers tighter around him, Sam tucked his feet under his blanket, but that didn't stop Maxie.

"Get up," Maxie insisted. "The parades are starting."

There was no use in resisting. Maxie might be mild-mannered most of the time, but when there was something he wanted to do — and watching parades with Sam was right up there — he didn't stop until he made it happen. Still, it was hard to move from the Technicolor dreamworld in which a smiling Heather tickled his foot to the steel gray morning, where the only things on the horizon were endless marching bands and New Year's parade floats covered with roses.

But as Sam dressed, after promising Maxie he would be downstairs as fast as humanly possible, he realized there *was* something to look forward to: life returning to normal. The thought surprised him. Usually, he was content to let vacations stretch on like pulled taffy. Soon school would start and Sam was pleased that it felt close enough to touch. This vacation had been nothing if not unsettling. Sam couldn't wait to leave behind all the tension that the holidays had brought, the questions about religion that seemed to have dotted almost every day of the past two weeks, and get back to more familiar irritants like homework and tests. Sam felt sure that God would not be making an appearance in the Hamilton Junior High cafeteria. Then, he flashed on the bearded old man on the mall escalator who had laughed just as Sam was tweaking God about Jupiter. That was just an old guy, right? Sam asked. You weren't pranking me, were You? A tree branch scratched against the windowpane, but Sam was not ready to take that as a sign of anything.

Enough of these one-sided conversations! Sam scolded himself. Concentrate on two-sided conversations, starting with Heather Daniels.

Heather. So, the foot tickling had been a dream, but she and Sam had spent some "quality time" together, as his dad liked to call it. How would that translate into seeing each other at school? Should he give her the big hello? Or wait for her to notice him? Perhaps he could just assume that, after their dance together, they were now friends. That was another thing his dad always said, Sam thought glumly: When you *assume,* you make an ass out of *u* and *me.* Sitting down at the edge of his bed, as much to steady himself as to tie the laces on his sneakers, Sam suddenly realized that if getting back to normal meant that Heather Daniels might be a part of things, then his life was not going to be very normal at all.

"Parades," Sam said aloud. Suddenly, parades were all he wanted to think about. Not the past couple of weeks, not the future. Just what was happening at that moment — and that was parades.

Pulling a sweatshirt over his head, Sam headed downstairs. Although a parade was blaring in the background, the rest of the house was kind of quiet, and Sam realized the discombobulation of the vacation wasn't over quite yet. New Year's Day had always had its own traditions. His mother and sister would take the ornaments off the tree and carefully pack them away while his father made chili to eat during the game. There was usually lots of joking around about this because, truth be told, Mr. Goodman's chili was not all that good. Every year, the family came up with ideas for improving the taste. Last year, Sam and Ellen had actually volunteered several bottles of spices they had purchased at an after-Christmas sale, but Mrs. Goodman thought some of the fallen pine needles would work just as well. In the past, she had suggested such other "seasonings" as lint from Mr. Goodman's oldest sweatshirt and paper from his shredder. Maxie always lobbied for candy. Every year Mr. Goodman pretended to have added some new secret ingredient to the mix to improve the flavor, but the chili always tasted the same. It was the silliness that was so delicious.

This morning, Mr. Goodman was in the kitchen, hauling out the pots and pans as usual, but with no tree to take down, Mrs. Goodman and Ellen were at loose ends. The menorah had been put away, and it had taken only a few moments to take down the holiday cards and wrap up their mother's new ornaments, which had been decorating the mantel. Ellen was sitting with Maxie, but she hated parades, always had, even as a kid, so she was doing her nails while she "watched."

"That stinks," Maxie said, wrinkling his nose and scooting down on the couch.

Ellen waved her hand in the air. "Sweet Strawberry," she informed no one in particular. "It's a great color. And you said you wanted company."

"It's not sweet, it stinks," Maxie repeated. "Even Pluto is hiding." He pointed to the dog, who was simply sleeping behind the couch like he always did.

"Fine. Here's Sam. He'll watch with you now." But when

Ellen got up, she didn't seem to know where to go. She headed toward the kitchen, but backed out when she saw her father putting on his apron.

"Where's Mom?" Sam asked.

"She's in the living room, reading," Ellen replied.

That was funny, thought Sam. Unless there was company, no one went in the living room. It got less living than any other room in the house.

Mr. Goodman poked his head out of the kitchen. "I'm about to start the chili."

None of the Goodman children said anything.

"Uh, do you want some breakfast before I start browning the meat?"

That was another New Year's Day joke. The kids always said they had to have something to eat before the kitchen started smelling of hamburger meat and chili powder.

"Sure," Sam said. He was hungry.

"I can make some French toast," Ellen suggested.

But just then, Mrs. Goodman appeared at the family room doorway. "That's all right, Ellen, I can make it."

Breakfast was an unsettling experience, too. Instead of everyone eating together, Sam and Maxie ate in front of the television, marching bands marching inexhaustibly before them, while their parents had their breakfast in the kitchen. Ellen just grabbed a bowl of cereal and said she had to pack for school.

Sam could hardly wait until Avi and his father came over to watch the football games. Usually, a bunch of people stopped by on New Year's Day, but this year when he'd asked his mother if they were having company, she'd snapped, "I didn't get around to asking anyone." She had looked at him as if she wanted to add, "You got a problem with that?"

People coming over might have been fun, but Sam was content with Avi and his dad. Now, however, sitting here with just them and his dad, watching football, it seemed kind of dead, despite the noisy game blaring from the television. Mrs. Goodman and Ellen had decided to go shopping since the mall was open, although what there was left to buy, Sam couldn't imagine. The guys sat gorging on chips and dip and avoiding the chili that was below par, even for Mr. Goodman.

"This game's a slaughter," said Mr. Cohen. He checked his watch. "We've got about a half hour until the next one."

Mr. Goodman got up and stretched. "Anyone for McDonald's?"

Sam and Avi hopped up off the couch. "Sure." They had been hoping some other food would appear. "Can we take Pluto?" Sam asked.

"Why not?" his father replied, putting on his coat. Pluto, hearing his name, jumped to attention and began pawing the door.

Everyone piled into the Goodmans' SUV. The temperature was in the mid thirties, at least, which for Chicago in January pretty much seemed like spring. Sam pulled off his stocking cap and shoved it in his pocket as he climbed in the back with Avi and Pluto.

"So, Avi," Mr. Goodman said, looking at the boys in the rearview mirror, "how's the bar mitzvah going?"

Sam rolled his eyes. Must his father have quality time with every kid who got into the car? But Avi didn't seem to mind. "I'm learning my portion of the Torah. I've pretty much got that down."

"Do you have a tutor? I remember my tutor, a skinny guy with a beard. Mr. Popovitch. He smelled like corned beef. I always got hungry studying with him."

Mr. Cohen laughed. "I'm Avi's tutor."

"Really?" Mr. Goodman said with surprise. "You know Hebrew that well?"

"I almost became a rabbi," Mr. Cohen responded. "But the more I studied, the more interested I got in ancient history, so I decided to get my Ph.D. instead."

"That must be nice, tutoring Avi," Mr. Goodman said almost wistfully.

"You'd have to ask Avi. Am I too stern a taskmaster?" Mr. Cohen turned to his son.

"You're okay," Avi said. "At least you don't smell like corned beef."

Sam knew his father had been bar mitzvahed — he'd seen a photo at Grandma Sally's house — but it was odd to think about. "Did you have a big bar mitzvah, Dad?" he asked.

"No. Certainly nothing like the ones today. There was a small lunch after the services."

Sam hesitated, but then he asked a question that had been on his mind. "Is Maxie really going to go to Hebrew school?"

"I don't know," Mr. Goodman answered curtly as he pulled into McDonald's drive-through.

Once they had their food, Mr. Goodman started talking to Avi's father about some case he was working on. Sam turned to Avi. It was the first chance they had had for a private word. "So what did you think of the dance?"

"It was pretty good."

"You danced with Vicki," Sam noted as he fed an eager Pluto a few french fries. "Twice."

Avi smiled, revealing ketchup on his braces. "Three times." Then his smiled faded, "What about you and Heather? Did she really want you to help her? You wouldn't tell me last night."

"I didn't want to get into it in front of the guys."

"So did she?"

Sam preferred to keep his private time with Heather private, even from Avi, so he said evasively, "Sort of. She didn't feel like dancing with Hank."

"Why not?" Avi asked with surprise. "Hank's a good guy."

"I'm not really sure," Sam replied. "Anyway, she had to go home early. Some party at her parents' house."

"Yeah, that's what you said." Avi hesitated. "Sam, do you really like her?"

Sam shrugged nonchalantly. "Sure, she's all right. What do you have against her?"

"She's a snob," Avi said bluntly. "She's not even polite. When I first came here, she was so rude to me. Once, I asked her to lend me a pencil, and she wouldn't. She didn't even look in her bag. She just said she didn't have one. And another time I asked about a history assignment, and she looked right through me."

"Well," Sam said slowly, "maybe she's not always the friendliest girl, but she can be nice when she wants to. She was last night."

Avi shook his head and took another bite of his burger. "It's your funeral."

"Hey, it's not like we're hooking up or anything."

"Like you wouldn't want to," Avi hooted.

Sam could feel a warm flush spreading across his face. "She's cute, okay? I think she's cute."

Mr. Goodman turned around in his seat.

"Who's cute?"

"Nobody!" Sam and Avi said in unison.

That night, after the games were over and Avi and his father had gone home, the Goodmans decided to spend the night at home playing Monopoly. Maxie wasn't a very good player, so he took turns playing with various family members. Tonight he wanted to play with his sister.

"I think we should buy Park Place, Ellen," Maxie told her.

"I do, too, Maxie, but first we have to land on it, remember?"

"Are you glad to be going back to school?" Maxie asked as he rolled the dice.

Ellen got a trapped look on her face. "Well, I'm going to miss everybody. But, sure, it'll be fun to see my friends at school. Aren't you looking forward to seeing your friends?"

"Yeah. I'm glad vacation is almost over. It wasn't too good."

Everyone looked over Maxie's head as he moved the little cast-iron dog marker six squares.

"Why do you say that, Maxie?" his mother asked gently.

Maxie looked up with surprise. "Because nobody was getting along," he said, as if that was so obvious, it hardly needed to be stated.

"Well, Maxie," Mr. Goodman said, clearing his throat. "It wasn't like we weren't getting along. It was just that with the Hanukkah bush gone, we were trying to find a different way to celebrate the season, and that led to some . . . disagreements."

Maxie frowned. "Celebrate. That means —"

"Have a good time," his father replied.

"But nobody had a good time," Maxie pointed out. "I didn't have a very good time. And Mom was crying, and the grandmas were fighting, and sometimes you and Mom were fighting —"

"Yes, sweetie, you have a point," Mrs. Goodman interrupted. "It's just that the holidays brought up a lot of feelings about which religion we want to practice in this house."

"*Practice* is the word," Ellen muttered.

"What do you mean by that?" Mrs. Goodman asked, an edge sharpening her tone.

"Well, Mother, you have to admit we only make these halfhearted attempts to do anything about religion. No one ever makes a commitment."

Uh-oh, Sam thought. Sometimes Ellen got a look in her eye and a sound in her voice that made it seem like she was the parent and their parents were the kids. It never led to anything good.

"Are you saying I don't know how I feel about God?" Mrs. Goodman asked, bristling.

"If you do, you've never communicated it to me," Ellen replied in a lofty tone.

"And am I to understand that you have strong feelings about God and religion? Because you've never really communicated those to me, either."

Ellen took a long sip of her cola. Then she said, "I'm drawn to the Eastern religions. Buddhism and Hinduism. Religions that don't believe in one god."

"Well, for your information, Ellen, I feel safety in the hands of a loving Jesus who protects and forgives me," Mrs. Goodman responded. "And I take comfort in the services of my church." She looked around defiantly at her family, as if waiting for someone to contradict her.

Mr. Goodman picked up the dice. "I think it's my turn to roll."

But his wife wasn't ready to let him off that easily. "However, you do bring up an interesting point, Ellen. Perhaps we haven't communicated our beliefs very well. For instance, I'm not sure how you feel about God, David. One minute you don't want anything to do with Judaism, the next you're talking about Maxie going to Hebrew school."

"He seemed interested," Mr. Goodman protested, still holding the dice.

"We've never even discussed a step like that."

"Look, Annie, if Maxie wants to go to Hebrew school, then I think we should encourage him."

"And who's going to take him back and forth to Hebrew school? You'll be at work."

"He's not old enough to go yet. Why are we even talking about this now?"

"I don't want to go to Hebrew school," Maxie interrupted, near tears.

Sam looked around the table, almost in shock. Usually, the one thing everyone in the family tried to avoid was upsetting Maxie. But now, his parents barely seemed to notice how distressed the kid was. His mother was pulling on her braid the way she always did when she was angry about something, and his father was rolling the dice around in his hand like he wanted to throw them across the room. Even Ellen had dropped the haughty demeanor and was simply staring at the wall, her arms folded, looking as if she were a Hindu yogi, willing herself somewhere else.

Sam wished he were somewhere else, too, but then a saying from the Bible popped into his mind. His mother said it whenever he and Ellen, or he and one of his friends, were having a fight: Blessed are the peacemakers. "Come on, you kids," she would say. "One of you end it. Blessed are the peacemakers."

"Hey!" Sam yelled, and slapped the table. "Quit it!"

"Sam!" His mother turned to him furiously. "What's gotten into you?"

"I'm being a peacemaker. We're blessed, remember?"

That broke the tension, at least temporarily. His mother stopped pulling on her braid and got up to get some more coffee. "David, do you want some?" she asked with a formal politeness.

"No, thank you."

When Mrs. Goodman returned, looking as though she had taken a few deep breaths, she said, "Sam, you were right to intervene. We've just been going around in circles here with our sniping." She turned to Ellen. "And you were right, too, my dear."

"I was?" Ellen said, surprised.

"Yes. Your father and I *haven't* made any commitments to our religion. No wonder you children are confused."

"I'm not *that* confused," Ellen muttered.

"Well, we're confused as a family."

"Why do we have to keep talking about this?" Sam asked belligerently. "I'm tired of it."

"Me too," agreed Maxie.

Mr. Goodman looked as if he wanted to say, "Me three," but he didn't.

Mrs. Goodman gazed around the table, taking everyone in. "We don't have to talk about religion and God anymore . . . for a while. But I'd like us all to be thinking about what we believe."

"Why?" Maxie asked.

"Because it's important to know where you get your comfort," Mrs. Goodman said simply.

"What if we come up with different conclusions? What if we don't agree?" Mr. Goodman asked, looking at his wife steadily.

"First let's think, then we can talk another day," she answered.

Well, thought Sam, at least they could all agree about that.

The Goodmans continued on with the Monopoly game, but everyone was just going through the motions. Yet no one was willing to say, "I quit." After the game finally ended, with Ellen and Maxie the winners, Sam said, "I think I'll take Pluto out one more time."

Mrs. Goodman looked at her watch. "It's late, Sam."

"It's nine o'clock," he said with exasperation. "I'll just walk down the block."

"All right," his mother agreed, "but just for a few minutes."

Sam called Pluto, asleep in front of the fireplace, where his soft snores mingled with the sound of logs quietly crackling. He roused himself, but everything about Pluto, from his expression to his body language, seemed to say, *Hey, I was comfortable and I don't have to pee. Let's forget it.* But Sam needed to get some fresh air. It was stifling inside.

Sam felt better the moment he got out of the house. It had

gotten colder, but the air was crisp, not frigid. Looking up, Sam could see tiny stars high in the sky, and a light mist of snowflakes making halos around the streetlights. As Sam walked with Pluto, ambling lazily alongside him, he noticed the small, perfect flakes falling on his jacket. There were so few, it was possible to see them individually before they melted.

Was it true, Sam wondered, that every snowflake was different? How was that possible? Of course, every person was different, so he guessed that it could be true of snowflakes as well.

Standing under a streetlight to see better, Sam caught a snowflake on his finger, then another. "Did You do that?" Sam asked aloud. "Make all the snowflakes and people, and maybe the stars, too, totally unique?" If everyone was special in his or her own way, maybe that's why God could be seen in so many ways. Seen through a billion pairs of eyes.

Sam looked up at the sky. "Is that right? Is that how it is?" There was no answer; this time, Sam didn't expect one. But the silence was soft, and it was comfortable.

CHAPTER
ELEVEN

Kids greeting one another, rushing through the doors, making their way through the crowded halls, banging lockers. Sam was glad to be back in school.

As he threw his coat into his messy locker, Sam felt relaxed, really relaxed, for the first time in days. He breathed in the particular odor of school — chalk dust, lemony disinfectant, grease from the cafeteria — all mixed together into something that smelled like normal.

Sam had only just turned toward his homeroom, ready to settle comfortably into the school day, when he bumped into Heather. Literally. His bent elbow jabbed into her arm, hard. There went the question of who was going to speak first.

"Ouch!" Heather cried, rubbing her hand along her forearm.

"Oh, gee, Heather, I'm sorry," Sam sputtered.

"You should watch where you're going."

His stomach, so relaxed just a moment ago, felt knotted into a bow.

"Nothing damaged, I guess," she said almost reluctantly.

Now what? Sam thought. Apologize again? Pretend like it hadn't happened and change the subject? But to what?

"So how was the rest of the dance?" Heather asked, breaking into his scattered thoughts.

Eagerly following her lead to somewhere beyond "ouch," Sam responded. "It was okay." Kind of boring once you left, was the unspoken message. She looked really nice today; her blond hair was back down, falling in waves to her shoulders. Once again, she was wearing red, this time, a thick woolly sweater. It reminded him of the red dress, only thicker and woollier.

"I wish I could have stayed," she said, turning her blue eyes on him. "Can you imagine anything worse than being stuck at home on New Year's with your parents and their friends?"

No, Sam thought feverishly. Plague, pestilence, nothing could be worse than that. Well, except being separated from Heather after rescuing her from the clutches of Hank Chin because of those same inconsiderate adults.

Heather looked at him expectantly.

Before Sam could stop himself, he heard himself saying, "I wish you could have stayed, too." Oh geez. Where was a sock when you needed one?

But Heather just smiled. Sam tried to read meaning into the slight uplifting of her lips, but she might as well have been smiling in Greek.

They turned into homeroom. Sam would have liked it to seem as if he was escorting Heather into the classroom, but she scooted ahead of him, and to anyone who was looking, it must have appeared as if he was simply walking into the room behind her. Not that anyone was looking. The rest of the kids were caught up in their own conversations about trips, presents, and the dance.

"Okay, okay, everyone take your seat," Mr. Tibold said as he strode into the room.

Jeremy objected. "The bell hasn't rung yet."

Mr. Tibold pointed at the clock, and the bell obediently rang. Less obediently, the class meandered to their seats.

Sam liked Mr. Tibold. Most of the kids did. He was young — still in his twenties, maybe, or, at the most, thirty — and he wore his thick brown hair pulled back in a ponytail. Sam wasn't too sure about the hairstyle. It reminded him of when his mother felt too busy to braid her hair and just wrapped a rubber band around it. But Mr. Tibold was easygoing, laughing at the kids' jokes, and was pretty tolerant of their high jinks. Mr. Tibold was also their history teacher, the class that came right after homeroom. Sam liked history, and English, too. Math was his worst subject. His parents always said they just expected him to do his best, but when it came to math, his best wasn't very good.

"So," Mr. Tibold said, rapping his desk for attention, "welcome back, everyone. I trust that you all had a good vacation."

"Awesome," Will called out.

"Well, that's good," Mr. Tibold said. "While I'm taking attendance, why don't you come up here and tell us all about it."

Some kids would have been embarrassed to be taken up on their wiseass comments, but not Will. Good looking, with an impressive head of dreads, Will was the star of the basketball team, and that prestige seemed to translate into everything he did.

Sauntering up to the front of the room, Will said, "I ate some fine food, I got a load of presents, I slept till I couldn't sleep anymore, and I went to a dance where it was all about me."

Most of the kids laughed, but there were a few catcalls.

"Not everyone seems to believe you, Mr. Jackson," Mr. Tibold commented while counting heads.

"Then they weren't at the dance," Will said with a wink as he went back to his desk.

Sam watched Will's performance with envy. A wink? Sam didn't know if he had ever offered anyone, much less a whole class, a wink.

"Anyone else want to catch us up on his or her holiday?" Mr. Tibold asked.

The rest of the class seemed to feel, like Sam, that perhaps it was better not to call attention to themselves.

"All right, then, let me read you a few announcements from the home office."

Sam's mind — and eyes — wandered over to Heather while Mr. Tibold read the welcome-back message from the principal and talked about the winter coat drive. What would she have said about her vacation? That a terrifically cool kid had helped her pick out a Christmas present and had rescued her at the dance? Or was he just a blip on her holiday radar screen?

Perhaps Heather felt Sam's piercing gaze; she turned around and looked at him and, unruffled, gave him that inscrutable smile once again. This time, Sam forced himself to smile back. It might have looked fake or maybe even more like a grimace than a grin, but he would not let himself look away until Heather turned her attention back to Mr. Tibold, who was reciting the new media center rules for using the Internet.

When the bell rang, some of the kids got up to go to the bathroom or hit the water fountain, but most stayed in their seats since they were all in Mr. Tibold's history class, anyway. Avi came over to Sam's desk. "Did I just catch Heather Daniels smiling at you?"

"Hey, keep it down," Sam whispered, even though there was no one within earshot.

"What's up?" Avi asked suspiciously.

"I don't know. She smiled, that's all."

"You smiled back," Avi noted.

"I think that's only polite, don't you?" Sam replied primly.

Avi just grunted.

"All right, everyone, let's settle down," Mr. Tibold said, leaning casually against his desk. "We've got a lot to talk about. We're starting a whole new curriculum in history this semester."

"The bell hasn't rung yet," Jeremy pointed out.

"Jeremy, we're only fifteen minutes into a new school year. You're trying my patience like it's April." He pointed to the clock, and the bell rang.

"As I mentioned before the break, we are going to be studying the Holocaust this semester, and we will be doing that in both social studies and English. Mrs. Hartnett will give you a reading list of books, and here, we'll be discussing the events that surround the Holocaust." Mr. Tibold paused. "I'm sure you're familiar with the term, but does anyone want to give me a definition of the Holocaust? Yes, Avi?"

"It was when the Nazis tried to kill all the Jews in Europe," he said quietly.

Mr. Tibold went to the blackboard and wrote "Holocaust."

"That's correct. The Holocaust is the umbrella term that is

used to cover the events surrounding the deaths of six million European Jews who were killed during the reign of Adolf Hitler. But other people were killed, as well — gays, Gypsies, and people with medical and physical infirmities."

Sam had heard about the Holocaust, of course, but he hadn't realized that so many Jews had been murdered. Six million? The number boggled his mind. And he hadn't known that other people had been targeted, too.

"We're going to do a lot of reading and discussion to try to find out why these terrible things happened, and why people let it happen. Does anyone have any initial thoughts on that?"

The class was quiet. Finally, Will raised his hand. "The people who did it were crazy?"

"Well, in one sense perhaps they were crazy. It can certainly be argued that anyone who wants to murder so many people is not normal. However, those in charge of the Third Reich, which was what Hitler's regime in Germany was called, had reasons they thought were perfectly logical. They thought that the Jews were at the root of Germany's social and economic problems."

Vicki raised her hand. "Why did the Germans think the Jews were to blame?"

"That's a good question, and we'll be studying the answers to it," Mr. Tibold said, "but does someone want to venture a guess?"

Another silence, but then Heather said, "Maybe they didn't like the Jews. They thought they were different or something."

Mr. Tibold nodded. "That was a part of it. I hope by the time we're finished with this project, you'll have a lot more answers. There is one more thing I'd like you to think about as you begin your studies. The Third Reich could not have carried out their plans without the help of many, many others — people who actively helped, and those who stood by and did nothing even though they may not have agreed with what the Third Reich was up to."

Ben O'Meara said, "You mean like regular people?"

"That's right," Mr. Tibold agreed. "Regular people. And not just in Germany, but in the other countries the Nazis controlled during World War II. Now, let me pass out the syllabus and I'll go over some of the material we're going to be studying. Next period, Mrs. Hartnett will give you the list of books you can choose from for your reports."

Mr. Tibold spent the rest of the class going over entries in the syllabus, and Sam tried to follow along. They were going to be studying the events that led up to Hitler coming to power, the decision to eliminate the Jews, the concentration camps, and stories from people who had survived the Holocaust. Sam felt his heart sink as he turned the pages. He wasn't sure he wanted to hear about any of this, it was so awful. His father was Jewish; so was his grandmother. If they had been in Europe during World War II, it would have been *his* family in danger.

As Sam gripped the syllabus, he couldn't help asking one more question: Why, God? Why?

His dark mood only deepened during English class. Mrs. Hartnett talked about the many books that had been written about the Holocaust. She said the whole class would read *The Diary of Anne Frank,* and then everyone would pick another book to read and share with the class.

Sam had heard about Anne Frank's diary. He even remembered when Ellen had read it, because she was so upset by it. She had cried about Anne, a Jewish girl from Holland who was forced to hide with friends and family in an attic. The Nazis had found them, anyway, and Anne had died in a concentration camp. It had been scary for Sam to think that someone his sister's age had had to hide and was killed; now, about Anne's age himself, the fear and agony seemed much closer.

By the end of Mrs. Hartnett's class, Sam was angry, but not just at the horrible things that had happened during the Holocaust. He was mad that the seventh grade was going to be studying it. One of the teachers, Mr. Tibold or Mrs. Hartnett, had said that teaching the Holocaust was mandated by the state of Illinois. That meant it was the law. What kind of law was that, Sam wondered, to make kids learn about such a stupid, horrendous, depressing thing?

He said as much to Avi while they were eating lunch in the cafeteria. Jeremy and Ben were arguing about some trade the Chicago Bulls had made for a point guard, but Sam wanted to talk about the Holocaust unit.

As he unwrapped the salami sandwich he had brought from home, Sam said, "I hope this Holocaust thing doesn't go on for too long."

"Why not?" Avi asked with surprise. "I think it sounds interesting."

"Depressing is more like it," Sam replied. "Doesn't it bother you, hearing about all those Jewish people who had to die?"

"It's not like I don't know about it. I've been hearing about it all my life."

Sam put his sandwich down. "What do you mean?"

"I had relatives who died in the concentration camps."

"But your family wasn't living in Europe, were they?"

"My grandparents had lots of relatives who were living in Poland. The Nazis rounded up Jews there, too. My grandmother had a sister who died, and my grandfather had cousins. Your dad is Jewish — maybe he had some family over there, too."

Sam had never heard about family members who died during the Holocaust. Had there been some? People his grandparents might have known who were unable to escape the Nazi claw? Wouldn't someone have told him?

When he arrived home from school, Mrs. Goodman was knitting by the fire. After she came home from school she always liked to take a half hour or so before she started making dinner, for, as she put it, a well-deserved rest. Sam sprawled out in front of the fireplace, warming himself next to the dancing flames.

"Mom, did anyone in Dad's family die in the Holocaust?"

Mrs. Goodman looked up from her knitting. "I don't think so. Why do you ask?"

"We're studying the Holocaust in school," Sam answered glumly.

"That's right," his mother replied thoughtfully. "Everyone has to study it in the seventh grade. I'd forgotten that you'd be doing it this semester."

"Avi had some relatives who died in concentration camps. Well, his grandparents' cousins or something. He said that maybe Dad had family who died, too."

"I've never heard anyone speak of it, Sam. Both of his parents were born in this country, but you'd have to ask him or Grandma Sally if there were any relatives left in Europe during the war."

Pluto, noticing Sam lying down at his level, plodded over,

stretched out, seemingly mimicked Sam's position, and gave him a slobbering kiss.

"Not now, Pluto," Sam said, pushing him away, but that didn't stop Pluto from coming at him once more with his frighteningly strong doggy breath.

"What kinds of things will you be studying?" Mrs. Goodman asked.

Sam quickly filled her in, how social studies and English were going to be combined, and how they were all going to read Anne Frank's diary. "Remember when Ellen read it, how upset she got?" Sam asked.

His mother put down her knitting. "I'm surprised *you* remember that."

"I don't know why we even have to do this unit. It's creepy," Sam said, throwing a rubber bone he had found on the floor to distract Pluto. It didn't work. Pluto nestled down right next to him.

"That's exactly why young people should study it, so no one ever forgets the horror that people can inflict on other people."

Sam sat up so he could better look into the shooting flames. Here we go again, he thought. People fighting one another, killing one another, and for what? Because someone didn't like the way somebody else looked or thought or believed. It didn't make any sense. So where were You this time, God? Sam asked belligerently. Where were You when that whole Nazi mess was getting started? Why didn't You do something before millions of people got killed? I mean, if You're so all-powerful, You ought to use that power to actually accomplish something. Saving Jews, and Gypsies, and gays, and people with handicaps might have been a good place to start. What were You so busy doing that could have possibly been more important than that?

CHAPTER
TWELVE

It was a question Sam was to wonder a lot about during the next several weeks. Like the fall of the Hanukkah bush, the seventh-grade Holocaust curriculum seemed to open lots of doors that had been firmly closed. Sam wasn't sure that they shouldn't have stayed shut.

Part of the unit was to talk to people who had lived through World War II, and ask what they remembered about the Holocaust. Some kids were making a big deal out of it; Vicki was going to the community center to interview senior citizens and play the tapes back in class. Sam figured it would be enough to talk to his grandmothers — though not to-gether, of course.

He asked his father to take him with him on one of his weekly visits to Grandma Sally. Sam used to go along on those trips a lot when he was younger; now, he preferred to sleep in. It was Maxie who regularly went into Chicago for the Sunday morning visits lately. He was mad when Mr. Goodman told him that he had to sit this one out.

"Why?" Maxie demanded.

Mr. Goodman sat down beside him on the family room couch. "Because Sam's going to be talking to Grandma about some sad things. You don't want to hear about sad stuff, do you?"

"Like what?" Maxie asked suspiciously. "You and Mom aren't getting a divorce, are you?"

Mrs. Goodman heard that. She practically bounded in from the kitchen. "Maxie, of course not."

"Are you sure?" Maxie insisted.

"Yes," his parents said, practically in unison.

"Then kiss."

Sam started laughing, which caused his parents to start laughing, too. "You sound like a boy emperor," Mr. Goodman said, but he got up, went over to his wife, threw her dish towel down on the floor, and gave her a real smooch.

Maxie was so pleased with himself that he forgot to ask anything else about the sad stuff that was going to be under discussion.

But in the car, heading toward Lake Shore Drive, Sam decided he wanted to talk about it himself before he got to his grandmother's. Why shouldn't he turn the tables on his father and bring up his own serious "car talk" for a change?

"Dad," he began, easing into the conversation, "it's not going to be easy to talk to Grandma about the Holocaust."

"I agree," his father said as he pulled onto the almost empty drive.

"I wish we weren't studying it," Sam said.

"I sort of wish you weren't, either," his father replied, keeping his eyes on the road.

Sam was surprised. "Why not?"

"It was one of the worst, most depressing periods in human history."

"Six million Jews died," Sam said.

"I know," his father replied quietly.

"Did you know about it when you were my age?" Sam asked.

"Of course. My parents would talk about it and there were movies I went to see when I was a little older than you." Mr. Goodman furrowed his brow, as if he were looking at something far away. "I remember blue-and-white cans with the Star of David that we used to collect money for Israel, so that the Jews would always have a safe place to live."

"It's not so safe now," Sam said, thinking about the ugly pictures he had seen on television of fighting in the Middle East.

"No, but at least we have a homeland."

Sam was surprised to hear his father say "we." It was the opening to the question he most wanted the answer to, but he waited a moment to ask it. "Did the Holocaust scare you when you were a kid?" he finally ventured.

Mr. Goodman turned to look at Sam. "Does it scare you?"

"I asked you first." Sam didn't want to sound like a wiseass, but he wanted to hear the answer before his father could turn the question back on him.

"Yes, it scared me," Mr. Goodman said, his voice heating up, "and it made me angry. I was mad at the Nazis and that devil Hitler, and at all the people who didn't do anything to help the Jews escape." Then he added wearily, "And in some ways, I was angry at the Jews, too."

"The people who died?" Sam asked with confusion. "But they were the victims."

"Yes, and I suppose it doesn't make much sense, but I hated thinking about people — my people — unable to protect themselves or fight back. That's what scared me most of all, I guess."

Sam remembered back to his last social studies class. "Sometimes they fought. We were just reading about the Warsaw Ghetto uprising, where the Jews in Poland fought back."

"Sometimes people fought valiantly. Mostly, there was no hope of fighting." Mr. Goodman sighed. "I always wondered what I would have done if they had come for me."

Suddenly, something occurred to Sam. "So is that why you don't like being Jewish?"

Mr. Goodman glared at Sam. "Who says I don't like it? I'm proud to be Jewish."

"But you don't —"

"Sam, don't be my psychiatrist. I'm happy I'm Jewish. Just because I don't go to synagogue regularly . . ."

Never, Sam thought.

". . . doesn't mean that I don't consider myself Jewish," said Mr. Goodman.

They rode in silence for a few minutes. "Sam, I just don't like the rules and regulations that religion — any religion — imposes, and I am not sure I believe in a God that lets things like the Holocaust happen."

Sam was tempted, so tempted, to ask his father what he did believe in. He had just about formed the words, when Mr. Goodman said, "Whoa, here's a parking spot, right in front of her apartment building. Get out, Sam. I'm going to have to parallel park and I'll be too close to the curb for you to open the door."

Oh well, Sam thought. Perhaps he didn't need to know the answer to that question, anyway. What if his father had said, "Nothing — *that's* what I believe in."

Sam wasn't sure what he believed in yet, but he was quite sure he believed in something. How could you talk to God if you didn't believe in Him?

And since Sam's class had begun studying the Holocaust, his talks with God had increased tenfold. They had social studies class every day, and practically every night, Sam was in his bed, tossing and turning and asking God questions, all depressing variations of the questions he had asked Him the day the Holocaust unit had begun:

How could You let this happen?

What did these people do to deserve to be dragged off to gas chambers?

Why didn't You just kill Hitler at birth?

How come nobody did anything to stop the Nazis — not until it was too late, anyway?

How could You let this happen?

Did God answer? Well, if not precisely answers, Sam was getting some information at school. Mr. Tibold was teaching the class about the reasons the Nazis came to power and why the Germans followed Hitler. And Sam was learning about how some people *did* try to stop Hitler, and how some people, at the risk of their own lives, helped the Jews and hid them from the Nazis. But why did God let the Holocaust happen? Sam still didn't have a satisfying answer to that question.

And, like his father, Sam wondered what he would have done if he had lived during the Holocaust. The question scared him, and so did any of the answers that came to mind.

Even though Grandma Sally didn't live in a retirement

home, it seemed to Sam as if most of the people in her building were old. Waiting for the elevator in her lobby, Sam noticed several elderly people sitting on the couch; one woman had her walker next to her, and a man had a portable oxygen machine. Had any of them lived in Europe during the Holocaust? Sam wondered. They might have been young at the time, maybe even his age. Sam knew that although so many people had died, others had lived through the horrible experience of being in the concentration camps. How was it possible to go on after something like that? Another question for God, Sam thought with a sigh.

When they got to his grandmother's apartment, Grandma Sally flung open the door with her usual enthusiasm. "Darlings," she said, kissing Mr. Goodman and practically smothering Sam with a hug. "Come in, come in. I've got bagels and lox, and kugel." She gave Sam a wink. "Apple and raisin today, Sammy, stuffed with apples and raisins."

Grandma Sally liked to stuff things, Sam thought. Her apartment was full to bursting. Photographs, artificial flowers, knickknacks were everywhere. There were hand-crocheted afghans over the back of the couch and two of the chairs. And paper! Newspapers, magazines, mail, and clipped articles that his grandmother liked to send to friends and family. She had even sent articles about video games to him and Maxie.

"Let's sit down, everything's prepared," Grandma Sally said, ushering Sam and his father to the table, which was nicely set with a lace tablecloth. "You're hungry, aren't you, Sam?" she asked as she bustled into the kitchen and came out with a tray of lox and bagels.

"Sure," Sam said. He had had some cereal for breakfast, but looking at the spread his grandmother laid out, his appetite was stoked.

Sam had fully intended to charge into his questions right away, but the food was so good, and his grandmother seemed so happy to see him, it didn't seem right to start talking about unhappy, long-ago events. So instead, the conversation jumped from school to Ellen and Maxie, and even to his mother and how things were going with the fourth grade.

"What about the dance, Sam?" Grandma Sally asked as she poured him some more milk. "Your father said you had a good time?"

"Yeah, it was fine." It seemed like a long time ago, really. Heather was still being friendly to him, but Sam didn't know how to move that into anything more. It wasn't as though the kids in his class actually dated. Usually, they hung around in a group. He just hoped that fate would somehow push them together again.

"The dance was fine," Sam replied again. He didn't want to get into too much detail.

"Did you dance?"

"Yes, I danced."

"I bet you were the belle of the ball," his grandmother said.

Sam was pretty sure that the belle of the ball was supposed to be a girl. "Well, I danced a little."

"Ma, I think Sam wants to talk to you about what it was like to live through the war," Mr. Goodman said, changing the subject. Sam shot his father a grateful look.

Grandma Sally shrugged. "I've lived through a lot of them. World War II, Korea, Vietnam, Gulf War I, Gulf War II."

"World War II," Sam clarified.

"Your grandfather fought in that war. He was only sixteen when he enlisted. He had to lie about his age to join up."

Sam looked at his father. "Sixteen?" That was only four years older than he was right now.

Mr. Goodman nodded.

"He wanted to fight the Nazis so badly," Grandma Sally continued. "I didn't know him then, but after we were married, he used to tell me he thought he would get to fight Hitler personally. After all that, he didn't even get sent to Europe. He fought in the Pacific."

Sam knew his grandfather must have been disappointed about not getting to take on the Nazis, but he felt a thrill of pride, anyway. He couldn't imagine being that brave.

"So what did you want to know about the war, Sam?" his grandmother asked, sipping her tea.

"I really want to ask you about the Holocaust."

Grandma Sally put her fork down. "Yes, I read that all the children have to study the Holocaust. That's good, very good. You know, we should never forget what happened."

Sam wasn't sure how to begin, so he plunged in with one of the questions he was very curious about. "Grandma, did you know anyone who died in the Holocaust?"

"Distant relatives who couldn't get out of Europe, but no one I had ever met," his grandmother responded. "I did know someone who lived through it."

"Who?" Sam asked with surprise.

"My cousin, Steve Geller."

"Steve? That was his name?"

"He changed his name once he got to America," Mr. Goodman said. "In Europe his name was . . ." He turned to his mother.

"Shlomo," Grandma Sally finished for him. "You were afraid of him, remember? Because he had numbers tattooed on his arm."

Sam had read that the concentration camp inmates had numbers tattooed on their arms by their captors. Those who had lived through the Holocaust had that mark the rest of their lives.

"No, I didn't like seeing those numbers," Mr. Goodman said uncomfortably.

"How did he get out of the camp?" Sam asked. "Was he liberated?"

"No, Steve didn't wait for that," Grandma Sally said. She leaned back in her chair. "This is a very gruesome story, Sam. Are you sure you want to hear it?"

Sam looked at his father. Did he? He wasn't sure.

Mr. Goodman shrugged. "It's up to you, Sam."

"I guess I do. What happened?"

"Steve was rounded up from the village in Poland where he lived, and was taken to Auschwitz." Sam felt himself flinch. Auschwitz was the most notorious of the concentration camps. "But he was a strong, healthy young man, so he was put on a work contingent. Well, the Nazis worked those men until they weren't so healthy anymore. One day, they took a pack of them out to clear a forest, and then when they were done working, the guards shot them."

Sam sat up in his chair. "But Steve wasn't shot?"

"No," Grandma Sally continued. "They kept some alive to dig the graves for the others. But, thanks be to God, while those other poor fellows were being murdered, Steve and a friend of his escaped."

"Escaped from the Nazis? How? Where did they go?"

"They ran through the forest and somehow found a farmer

who was willing to hide them. The man kept them for a while until it became too dangerous, then he helped them get to Russia, where the Russians were fighting the Germans. They joined the Russian army, and when the war was over, Steve and his friend came to the United States."

Sam found he had been holding his breath. The story was both terrible and wonderful, in a way — Steve had escaped, someone had helped him and his friend survive, and he had made it to Chicago. "Wow," Sam said. "I can't imagine how Steve got the nerve to just run into the forest to escape the Nazis."

"It took courage," Grandma Sally conceded, "but he really didn't have anything to lose."

"You see, Sam," his father said, "after he dug the graves, the Nazis would have shot him, anyway."

Sam sat at the table trying to take that in. He could almost see it, Steve digging in the soft, mossy ground of the forest with bodies piled up around him. Then, when there was room enough for everyone —

"Are you all right, Sam?" his father asked. "Maybe Grandma shouldn't have told you about Steve."

"No, I wanted to know," Sam said quietly. That was one of the purposes of talking to people about the Holocaust: so you would remember their stories.

As his grandmother reached over to pat his hand, lightly,

not like her usual enveloping touches, Mr. Goodman said, "Maybe we should be getting home."

"Not yet," both Sam and Grandma Sally said at nearly the same time.

"All right," Mr. Goodman said restlessly, "then I'm going to take a walk. I'm stuffed, and I want to stretch my legs."

After Mr. Goodman closed the door, Grandma Sally sighed. "He never could listen to stories about what the Jews suffered during the Holocaust."

"It *is* kind of scary," Sam admitted.

"Would you like to see a photo of Steve?" Grandma Sally asked.

Sam nodded, so Grandma Sally got up and pulled a black leather photo album out of her bookcase. She motioned to Sam to join her on the couch, and she leafed through the pages until she found one of Steve.

Sam peered at the old snapshot. There was nothing re-markable about Steve. In the picture he was middle-aged, thin, slightly balding. What struck Sam was that he had a big smile on his face. Sam thought if he had gone through the things Steve Geller had, he might never have smiled again.

"Steve did very well for himself when he got to America," said Grandma Sally. "First he owned a fish store, and then he started dabbling in real estate. He owned several buildings when he died."

"He's dead?"

"A couple of years ago. He died suddenly, in his sleep."

All that, and then just to die in his bed one night. Sam shook his head. Turning to his grandmother, he asked, "How could all that terrible stuff happen?"

Grandma Sally put her arm around Sam's shoulder. "I don't know, sweetheart."

"Where was God? What was He doing when so many people were getting tortured and murdered?"

"He was watching. He saw it all."

"Just watching?"

"Watching and crying, Sammy. Watching and crying."

CHAPTER THIRTEEN

Sam knew he shouldn't have waited to start this reading assignment. All he had to do was choose one book from the Holocaust reading list and write a report on it. Last week, there had been plenty of books on the shelf at the school library, but by the time Friday had rolled around, there was almost nothing. After complaining to his mother, who, of course, had wondered why he'd waited until Friday, Mrs. Goodman suggested he spend Saturday morning at the public library. But now that he was here, it was clear the pickings weren't much better. The librarians had thoughtfully put aside a shelf for the Holocaust books to accommodate the seventh graders in Evanston who were studying the subject, but everything Sam wanted to read was among the missing.

"*Number the Stars*," Sam mumbled as he checked first his list, then the shelf. "Gone."

"*The Devil's Arithmetic.*" That sounded interesting, Sam thought. Not there. After a few more tries, Sam finally just grabbed a book from the shelf. *Mischling, Second Degree* was the title. He didn't even know what that meant, but it was a book from the list. Heading down the long wooden staircase to the checkout desk, Sam could see that the line was long, so he decided to browse in the AV room for a while and maybe find a DVD — a stupid, mindless comedy that required no thought — to take home. Instead, he found Avi and Vicki sitting at one of the tables, deep in conversation.

"Hey guys," he said, ambling over to them. "What's up?"

Sam thought Vicki looked a little disappointed at the interruption, but Avi gave him a big hello. "Sam, guess what? Vicki's having a party tonight."

"A party? Cool." Sam's hopes soared. The word "party" meant one thing to Sam: Heather.

"It's a sleepover," Vicki corrected.

"So that means it's for girls," Sam said with disappointment.

"Well, yeah." Vicki gave him the "duh" look.

"But guys can come over before the sleeping part starts," Avi put in. "Five guys."

Sam pulled out a chair and plopped himself down.

"Because you've got five girls?"

Vicki rolled her eyes. "Sam, get with the program. Five girls, five guys. I'm trying to figure out which boys Avi should bring with him."

Who cared which boys were going to be there? Sam thought. "What about the girls?"

Vicki ticked them off on her fingers: "Me, Anna, Carrie, Heather, and Britt."

Sam hadn't been aware that he was holding his breath until he let it out once Vicki said Heather's name.

"I don't like Heather much, either," Vicki said, looking between Avi and Sam, "but I wanted Britt to come, and this year Britt and Heather are best friends. . . ." Vicki's voice trailed off. Seventh-grade friendships could be very complicated.

Sam didn't care why Vicki didn't like Heather as long as she was going to be there. "So what time should we show up?" he asked buoyantly.

"First the rest of the guest list," she insisted. "You . . ." she began, then shifted her gaze shyly to Avi, "and you —"

"Jeremy," Sam added promptly.

Vicki thought about it.

"What?" Sam said indignantly. "Jeremy's our friend."

"Jeremy can be so rude. . . ." She looked over at Avi, who shrugged. "Invite whoever you want, Vicki."

"Well, I want Will, that's three, and okay, Jeremy —"

"And Ben O'Meara," Sam finished the list for her. "You like Ben, right?"

"Yeah, and I think Britt might have a thing for Ben."

Sam wondered if Heather might have a thing for *him*. Maybe he would find out tonight. This party was shaping up just fine, Sam gloated. Ben and Britt, Avi and Vicki, he and

Heather. Jeremy, Will, Carrie, and Anna could just figure it out for themselves.

Sam glanced up at the clock. He needed to get home. "What time should we be there?"

"My mom said I could have the boys over from seven-thirty to nine-thirty. So that means you can probably stick around until ten."

"Okay," Sam said, getting up. "What about getting there?"

Avi nodded. "I'll ask my dad if he can drive us."

It was a happy Sam who checked out his library book, and then pushed the heavy library doors through to the outside. A blast of January cold hit him so fast, his ears were turning red by the time he pulled his stocking cap out of his pocket and got it on. Even the frigid temperature couldn't dampen Sam's spirits. There was a wonderful feeling rolling around inside him, and as he strode along, he tried to put a name to it. Ah, yes, anticipation.

The bus stop was a couple of blocks from the library, through Evanston's downtown — a real one, with shops, restaurants, and movie theaters. It was a place where Sam and his friends sometimes hung out, but the mall was more conducive to having fun; besides, it was cool in the summer and warm in the winter.

Sam was tempted to stop in one of several coffee places and get a hot chocolate for the ride home, but his bus was waiting, its motor running and gray exhaust pluming from its tailpipe. With no frothy drink with which to warm himself, Sam tried to find the least cold part of the bus so he could concentrate and figure out what to tell his parents about this evening. Doing boy-girl stuff was so new, he wondered what exactly he should say. They had made such a big deal about the dance, he definitely wanted to play this night down. He considered his words and defined his attitude. By the time he walked into the house, Sam had his game plan ready. Tonight was about just a few friends getting together. Nothing to get excited about. In by 7:30, out by 10.

And who knew what fun stuff in between.

"Hey, what are you doing here?" Sam asked as he came into the family room.

Ellen was lying on the couch with Pluto curled up at her feet, but he sprang up upon seeing Sam, and began barking.

"Quiet, Pluto! I had a toothache," Ellen mumbled. "So I got a ride in from Madison, and Mom took me right to the dentist."

"Are you okay?"

"The novocaine's wearing off. It hurts, but I'll live." She sat up slightly. "What's going on around here?"

Sam plopped down on a chair. "Not much."

"Everybody getting along?"

"I guess," Sam said slowly. Things had pretty much gotten

back to normal. But his mother had gone to church every Sunday since vacation ended, which was something new. Sam filled Ellen in on that bit of news.

"How's Dad reacting?" Ellen asked.

Sam shrugged. "Okay, I guess. He just goes to Grandma Sally's like always," he informed his sister. "He didn't even say anything when Mom asked me to go to church with her tomorrow. She and Nana are going to that big church in Chicago."

"St. James Cathedral? How come?"

"Mom just said she and Nana like to go there sometimes, it's a good place to experience a service."

Ellen swung her feet off the couch, annoying Pluto, who jumped down and padded over to his favorite spot in front of the fireplace.

"Are you going?"

Sam had been taken off guard when his mother had asked him to go to church. He'd been setting the table for dinner on Friday night, his mind on nothing more than trying to remember on which side of the knife to place the spoon, when his mother casually asked, "So are you still thinking about religion these days, Sam?"

"Uh, sometimes," he'd answered in his best neutral voice.

"Now that I'm going to church more often, why don't you come with me one Sunday?"

Sam's first thought was of his father, but to his mother, he just gave a noncommittal nod.

"What about this Sunday? I'm meeting Nana downtown." His mother had looked both vaguely guilty, as though she knew she was putting him on the spot, and determined, as well.

"Mom really seemed like she wanted me to go," Sam told Ellen, "and I needed to talk to Nana, anyway. I'm supposed to interview people who lived through World War II for my Holocaust unit."

Ellen nodded. "Oh yeah, seventh grade."

"So that's one of the assignments. I went over to Grandma Sally's last week. And, El, it was weird. Dad couldn't get out of her apartment fast enough. He wanted to leave even before she was finished talking."

"Really?" Ellen said thoughtfully.

"Hey, did you know we had a relative who was a prisoner in a concentration camp?"

"Steve somebody?"

"Yeah. How come you knew and I didn't?"

"I remember him. He was over at Grandma Sally's a couple of times, but I was pretty young. You were just a toddler."

Maxie came into the room just then, so that ended the conversation, but Sam allowed himself to sulk for a few moments as he pondered why so many things in this family were hidden from view. His view, anyway.

Sam was determined to wait for just the right moment to ask for permission to go to the party, but as the afternoon progressed, it never presented itself. Avi, calling to say the ride for tonight was a go, was appalled that Sam hadn't yet checked with his parents. But whenever Sam tried to talk to his mother, she was on her way to the knit shop, or needed to get to the cleaners before it closed, and his father was later than usual getting home from his Saturday at the office. Finally, with the fire roaring in the family room, Mr. Goodman was settled in with the newspaper and Mrs. Goodman was sitting in her favorite spot knitting. The scene was so cozy, Sam hated to interrupt, but if he waited much longer, Mr. Cohen would be pulling into the driveway.

"Mom, Dad . . ." Both of them looked up. "Can I go out tonight?" he finished in a rush.

Mrs. Goodman looked at him curiously. "Where do you want to go? Avi's?"

That was Sam's usual Saturday night haunt. "Well, Avi's going to be there. . . ."

"Where's there?" Mr. Goodman asked. Clearly, he felt something suspicious was going on.

"Uh, Vicki Freeman's having a party. A slumber party. Well, that's for the girls, I mean the sleepover part. . . ." Sam could hear himself starting to babble. This wasn't going quite the way he had hoped.

"Sam, sit down and start from the beginning," his mother said, patting the seat on the couch next to her.

"Okay," Sam said, but he remained standing. "I ran into Vicki and Avi at the library, and she said she was having a sleepover, but that her parents said a couple of us guys could come over for a couple of hours."

"How many are a couple and how long is a couple?" Mr. Goodman asked.

"Five guys and two and a half hours."

His parents looked at each other. "That sounds reasonable," Mrs. Goodman said. "Are you sure Vicki's parents are going to be home?"

"I guess."

"Well, I'll call Mrs. Freeman and find out the details."

"Mom! You can't call, that's so lame."

Mrs. Goodman, who had put down her knitting to give her full attention to Sam's mumblings and stumblings, now picked it up again. "I don't call, you don't go," she said, her needles clacking.

Sam looked at his father helplessly, but he just shrugged.

"All right," a defeated Sam said, "call. But then I can go, right?"

"After I talk to Vicki's mother, we'll see." His mother put her knitting down once more and went into the kitchen to phone Mrs. Freeman.

That left Sam and his father sitting together in silence, though not for long. "So Sam, it seems girls are getting to be a bigger part of your life lately."

Was his father going to go into sex ed mode every time he said hello to someone of the opposite sex? The next decade was going to seem awfully long if that was the case. Before Mr. Goodman could continue, Sam looked straight at his father and said, "Dad, please, I'm just going over to Vicki's with a couple of the guys and we're going to hang around. For two and a half hours. That's it. No big deal. Okay?" He said "okay" so loudly, it surprised him.

Mr. Goodman looked startled as well. "Okay." He buried himself back inside his newspaper.

Sam wondered what was happening with the phone conversation in the kitchen, but he didn't want to be caught eavesdropping. After what seemed like an eternity but in reality was only a few minutes, his mother reappeared.

"You can go," she said, not prolonging the suspense. "Mrs. Freeman is going to be home, and you have to be out by ten. As she settled back on the couch, Mrs. Goodman asked casually, "What are you going to wear?"

Oh no, not again. He was not going to be like Ellen and start ripping through his closet for the perfect outfit every time he had to show up someplace where the opposite sex was on the premises. Nope. Not happening. "Jeans. And a sweater or something." He looked at his mother defiantly, daring her to make a suggestion.

"Sounds good," she said, counting her stitches. Sam thought maybe he saw a hint of a smile, but it came and went so quickly, he wasn't sure.

When it actually came time to get ready, however, Sam put a lot more thought into his outfit than he would have cared to admit. The brown sweater he had received for Hanukkah? He checked himself out in the mirror. It seemed so . . . so brown. And maybe it was too dressy. He pulled the sweater off and tossed it on his bed. A sweatshirt would be a better choice, but after spending a few frustrating minutes pawing through his drawers, he found his Wildcats sweatshirt crumpled up on the floor of his closet behind his laundry basket.

Great. Now what? Sam could feel himself starting to get hot and sweaty, perhaps from changing clothes and crawling around in the closet, but maybe a touch of agony was causing his face to flush as well. What *was* he going to wear?

Ellen stuck her head in the doorway. "Hey, Mom and Dad are going out. I'm supposed to pick you up after the slumber party. So be ready at ten. Outside."

"It's not a slumber party, and you know it," Sam said, flinging around a few clothes.

"Having a clothes crisis?" she asked, stepping into the room.

"No," Sam said with a scowl.

Ellen walked over to the closet, pushed aside a few articles of clothing, and pulled out a denim shirt. "That's it. Clean, casual, seems as if you don't care, but still looks good."

Sam took the shirt from his sister. She was right. It would be perfect. "Thanks," he mumbled.

"See you at ten. Outside. Don't make me wait."

Thinking ahead, Sam had brought his coat upstairs with him so he could put it on and avoid running the gauntlet of his parents' scrutiny. No pictures with Pluto this time. So when Avi's dad honked the horn at precisely 7:20, Sam was ready to move quickly out the door. "Bye," he said as he hurried through the family room.

"Hold up," Mr. Goodman said.

"Mr. Cohen is waiting," Sam protested.

"Just a second," Mrs. Goodman said, pulling him close for a quick hug. "Have a good time."

"I will."

"And don't do anything stupid," Mr. Goodman called from his chair.

"What could that be?" Sam asked. "We're practically going to turn around and go home as soon as we get there."

"Two hours can be longer than you think," his father responded.

If Mr. Goodman seemed wary about the evening's events,

Mr. Cohen was positively upbeat. Sam didn't know which attitude was more disconcerting. "So are you boys going to have a great time tonight?" Mr. Cohen asked enthusiastically as he pulled out of the Goodmans' driveway. Sam and Avi exchanged looks. How were they supposed to know?

"I hope so," Sam finally said politely.

"Well, I hope so, too," Mr. Cohen said. "What are you going to do?"

That was another question Sam had wondered about since that afternoon. What *would* they do? "Just hang out," he told Mr. Cohen. That should cover just about everything.

Before Sam had time to get too nervous, they were at Vicki's house.

"Ellen's going to pick you up, right?" Mr. Cohen said as they got out of the car.

"Yes." Sam wished that the day when he could just drive himself places wasn't so far away.

Vicki's house was a split level with a big rec room in the basement. Mrs. Freeman greeted the boys and took their coats. "The girls are all here," she said as she ushered them downstairs.

Sam felt the same butterflies fluttering in his stomach that had been there the night of the dance. They calmed down a little when the first faces Sam saw were Jeremy's and Ben's. The girls, huddled together on the corduroy couch off in the corner, were giggling and whispering. They waved and said hi when the boys walked in, but none of them made a move — not Vicki, and certainly not Heather.

"Hey, what's up?" Ben asked as he grabbed a cola from a table laden with soft drinks, pretzels, and chips.

"Not much," Sam said, and Avi nodded. "Not much."

There seemed nothing to do but take their place standing at the refreshment table and scarf down snack food, but Sam wasn't even hungry.

Then, with all the energy of someone who had done handsprings down the stairs, Will appeared. "Hey, everybody," he said in a booming voice. Then he looked around. "What's going on? Boys here, girls there? Fugetaboutit. Let's all move to the center of the room, shall we?"

Sam and Avi exchanged looks. There was Will, Mr. Personality. He was never shy, that was true, but tonight he had morphed into a TV host or something. Amazingly, the girls were responding to Will's taking charge. They got up and moved to the middle of the room, where the arrangement of couches and chairs forced them to spread out a little.

Then Will sat down between Anna and Heather. He motioned the other guys over; they brought their drinks and sat down, too.

"How about some music?" Will said, turning to Vicki, who looked glad to have something to do.

"Sure," she said, popping up and heading over to the CD player.

Sam wished that Will wasn't sitting so close to Heather, but he was glad someone had taken the initiative to get them all together. But now what? Will seemed to have that covered, too. "So, I've got a plan. Something we can do tonight," he began.

Carrie, who was small and dark and full of impish fun, just laughed at Will. "Oh, you do? Who died and left you boss?"

"We can sit around and watch TV, or we can do something interesting," Will informed her.

"My parents are right upstairs," Vicki reminded him nervously as she came back to the couch.

"And if they come down, all they'll see us doing is talking," Will assured her.

"Where are you going with this, man?" asked Jeremy.

Will looked around the room with sly expectancy. "Let's play Truth or Dare!"

Truth or Dare, the game where someone had to tell the truth to some embarrassing question or else agree to whatever dare was proposed. The kids exchanged furtive looks with one another. Sam could tell that most of them felt like he did: Truth or Dare sounded like fun — and a little bit dangerous.

Heather spoke up first. "I don't know. It might be okay. It sounds kind of interesting."

Once Heather broke the ice, Britt followed her lead. "Yeah, it does sound interesting. If everyone agrees to tell the truth."

"Oh, you have to be totally honest," Will said, "or there's no game. Everyone agree to that?"

There were mumbled assents.

Ben went over to the refreshment table and brought back a bowl of chips and plopped them down. "So what are the rules of this game, Will, since you seem to know all about it?"

"I know how to play," Heather jumped in before Will could answer. "Everyone puts his or her name in a hat —"

Glaring at her, Will interrupted. "And then, one by one we all pull a name. Like, if I pick Heather, I say, 'Truth or dare.' If she picks truth, Heather has to answer a question — *honestly*, like we said. Dare, she has to do whatever I tell her to."

"Anything?" Sam asked.

"Get your nose out of the gutter, Goodman," Will said, laughing. "Anything within reason."

"That's not what I was thinking," Sam said indignantly. Geez, he was just trying to get the rules of this game straight. Heather smiled at him, anyway.

"Get paper and pencils," Will directed Vicki. He turned to Jeremy, who was wearing his baseball cap. "Marcos, give me your hat."

As Vicki was gathering the Truth or Dare paraphernalia,

Mrs. Freeman came down the stairs carrying a platter of cookies. "Some more fuel for you kids," she said brightly.

"Thanks, Mom," Vicki said.

"Why aren't you dancing?" Mrs. Freeman asked as she put the cookies down on the coffee table in front of the kids.

"Mom," Vicki said in an aggrieved voice.

"All right, I'm going. Have fun."

When her mother was out of earshot, Vicki said nervously, "Maybe this isn't such a good idea."

"Oh, it'll be fine," Anna said. "Like Will said, Truth or Dare looks perfectly innocent."

Sam felt a few qualms as he wrote down his name, but everyone else seemed to be writing down names and throwing them into the hat with enthusiasm.

"I'll go first," Will said. He read the name and said with a grin, "Goodman." Sam's heart sank. Did he have to be first? He wasn't ready, but there was no way out.

"Okay, my man," Will said, dramatically pointing a finger at Sam. "Truth or dare?"

Sam debated with himself. Who knew what question Will might come up with to embarrass him? It might be easier to do some insane stunt. "Dare," Sam said, trying to sound non-chalant.

Will pulled a cookie from the platter and chewed it

thoughtfully. You could have heard one of the crumbs drop until he finally said, "I dare you to go in the laundry room with Heather for five minutes."

All the kids laughed and hooted. Sam shot a glance at Heather, who looked cooler than he felt. "That's a dare for both of us," he noted.

"I don't mind," Heather said, getting up. Sam had no choice but to follow her into the laundry room. Not that he didn't want to, but with everyone's eyes on him, he felt like an actor onstage.

"We'd better close the door," Heather said.

Sam closed it. Now what?

"Boy, I never thought I'd be grateful to Will Jackson, but I'm glad we got some time by ourselves," Heather said.

"Me too," Sam said, surprised, excited, and afraid all at once.

An extended silence followed.

"So what do you want to do?" Heather finally asked, licking her lips a little.

Well, what *could* they do surrounded by dirty laundry in baskets?

"Uh, we could talk?" Sam suggested.

"Talk?" Heather wrinkled her nose. "What about?"

Sam was caught in a whirlpool of emotions. He wasn't doing this right. He was alone with Heather — albeit in a laundry room — something he had been thinking about for weeks. Here was Heather, looking great in tight jeans and a pink sweater, and she seemed like she might want to kiss him. Him! Sam Goodman! And he was standing around talking about talking. . . .

Before he could figure out what to do, Heather walked over to him, put her arms around his neck, and kissed him right on the lips. He wasn't sure, but he thought he kissed her back.

"There," she said with satisfaction. "Let's go back out."

"We can't," was all a shocked Sam could think of to say. "We still have about four minutes."

Heather considered that and then hopped up onto the top of the washer. "You're right. We don't want to get out there too soon."

If it had been left to Sam, they probably would have stood there for the next four minutes without uttering a word, but the kiss didn't seem to faze Heather a bit. She pulled a pack of gum out of her jeans. "Want one?" she asked.

Dumbly, Sam took a stick. It was too late to worry about bad breath, he supposed, but still.

Heather flipped her hair over her shoulder. "I'm glad we got that over with," she said. "If we're going together, that's probably all you'd be thinking about, when you could try to kiss me. So now it's done."

They were going together? Sam really felt he had to say something. "I . . . I —"

Heather held up a flannel nightgown dotted with hearts, which had to belong to Vicki. "Ugh, this is so babyish." She turned her attention back to Sam. "Anyway, I kind of liked you ever since you helped me pick out Jeremy's present."

"You did?" There, he'd said something.

"And then you got me away from that dork Hank Chin at the New Year's dance." Heather gave Sam one of her megawatt smiles. He hardly noticed that she blew a small bubble with the gum before she closed her mouth.

"Well, I was glad to help out," Sam said, although he wished Heather hadn't characterized Hank as a dork. He had always seemed a good enough guy. Why *did* Heather think he was a dork? Instead of just responding to questions, Sam was ready to ask that one when Heather tossed the nightgown aside and said, "Those hearts remind me of something. Valentine's Day is almost here."

Wasn't it still January? "Not for a couple of weeks, right?" Sam said timidly.

"You know the date, don't you?" Heather said coyly.

All Sam remembered was that Valentine's Day was in the middle of February. It wasn't a date that had loomed large on his calendar, although it appeared now that it was going to. "Yes," Sam lied, "I know the date."

"Good," Heather said, flashing another smile. "Maybe there'll be another dance."

"That would be good," Sam said. Then, screwing up his courage, he asked, "Maybe we can, like, go to it together. If there is one."

Heather jumped down from the washer. "Yeah, of course." She looked at her watch. "It's gotta be five minutes now."

Trying not to think, and afraid that he was moving in that stiff way that characterized a robot — or Frankenstein — Sam nonetheless walked himself over to Heather. Although unsure where to put his hands or, for that matter, his nose, he edged himself as close as he could to her and caught her on the side of the lips with a kiss of his own. It wasn't very impressive, he knew. His grandmother's kisses lasted longer than that one, but with the satisfaction of a job completed, Sam stepped aside and let Heather lead the way back into the room.

"Hey man, we thought you got lost in there," Will greeted him.

"You were *so* holding up the game," Carrie said with a smirk.

Sam looked at Avi, who didn't say anything, but who had, Sam noticed, moved next to Vicki.

"If I would have known that dare was going to be so fun," Will said, frowning, "I wouldn't have given it to you." He didn't seem to be having as good a time as he had before he'd sent Heather and Sam to the laundry room.

Sam just tried to stay — and look — cool. It was no one's business what went on in the laundry room, though from the way Heather was exchanging glances with Britt, it seemed like it might be Britt's business soon. "Dare completed," Sam said. "Whose turn is it now?"

The game went on. Britt picked Vicki, who chose truth.

"Name the person you would want to be your first boyfriend. Someone you know, or a star," Britt said, knowing she was putting Vicki on the spot. If she didn't say Avi, he'd be hurt, but if she picked Avi over any of her celebrity crushes, that would prove that her feelings were deep.

"Avi," Vicki said promptly, acting as if it was no big deal. There was almost as much hooting and laughing as when Sam and Heather had been sent to the laundry room.

Carrie picked Avi's name out of the hat next, and when he picked truth, she just shrugged and smiled. "Same question."

Sam didn't even have to listen to know that Avi would say Vicki. He was such a nice guy that, even if he would have preferred a celebrity, he wouldn't hurt Vicki's feelings after she had just put herself on the line for him.

After that, Carrie and Will both took dares. Carrie had to call Mr. Tibold and pretend that she was an old girlfriend. She tried, but she giggled so much, she had to get off the phone before she made much sense. Will was supposed to call Miss Larkin, the curvy athletics coach, with the same ruse, but she wasn't home, and he got the answering machine. Some of the kids thought he should have to make another call, but Will successfully argued that he had taken the dare, and shouldn't be penalized just because Miss Larkin wasn't home.

Then it was Avi's turn to pick a name. "Heather," he said. "Truth or dare?"

Heather tossed her hair and said, "Truth."

Avi looked at her thoughtfully, "So why did you want to be rescued from Hank Chin at the dance?"

Sam aimed a surprised look at Avi, then he glanced back at Heather, who seemed thrown by the question. "I . . . I was just tired of dancing with him."

Britt rolled her eyes. "You're supposed to tell the truth."

Jeremy jumped on that. "Hey, Heather, no fair cheating."

"I'm not cheating," she responded, glaring at Britt. "If you must know, I just felt uncomfortable with Hank."

"Why?" Avi asked.

"Because I did," Heather said. "I just did. That's the truth," she practically spat the words at Avi.

"Oh, come on, Heather," Britt said giddily. "Do your imitation of Hank, where you pull your eyelids up and talk with that fake accent."

Heather's face reddened, and her mouth twisted. "Stop making things up, Britt."

Britt looked surprised as she took the full force of Heather's irritation. "Sorry," she muttered.

Heather didn't look very attractive now, Sam had to admit to himself. He wanted her to go back to looking as pretty as she had in the laundry room. "Hey," he heard himself say, "this game is getting dumb. Why don't we quit and listen to some music?"

Heather turned toward Sam and smiled her appreciation, her gratitude softening her features.

There, that was better.

CHAPTER FOURTEEN

It wasn't one of Sam's restful nights. Every time he dozed off, his sleep was plagued with dreams, none of them memorable, but all of them unsettling. Finally, as the gray morning light filtered into his room, Sam decided to get up.

Throwing off his tangled covers, Sam made his way to the bathroom that he shared with Maxie, trying hard to not disturb his softly snoring brother, whose door was open. Even though the heat had kicked on during the night, the house was so cold that once he'd finished in the bathroom, he fled back to his bed and huddled under his comforter. Now what? The thought of going downstairs to surf the Net made him shiver, and if he turned on his radio, he'd wake everyone up.

Did he want to lie in bed and think about kissing Heather? No, he did not. Sam was sure there would come a time when he might enjoy going over every detail, but now the memory seemed too big and too near.

So what did that leave? He was in too good a mood to quiz God. But thinking of God reminded Sam that he still had that book to read for the next week. Reading for a while wouldn't be so bad, and the best part was that his backpack was right next to his bed. He barely had to roll over and he had the book in his hand.

Sam turned on his bedside light and settled in with *Mischling, Second Degree*. Scanning the flap to see what the book was about, Sam was at first surprised, then agitated at what he was reading. Apparently, a German girl named Ilse was in danger because she was part Jewish — and only a small part: Her grandmother was a Jew. Sitting up, Sam turned the pages quickly, trying to learn more. Her parents kept the truth from her because if anyone discovered her family background, she'd be treated like any other Jewish girl in Hitler's Germany. Sam pulled his comforter more tightly around him. He was shaking, and it wasn't just from the cold.

Why had it never occurred to him? As horrible as the events of the Holocaust were, Sam had never thought of them in conjunction with him, not personally. Of course, it had been frightening to think about what would have happened to his dad or grandmother, or Avi, had they been living in Europe during Hitler's time in power. There had been moments when Sam had pictured people he cared about being rounded up and taken away; beyond that, he wouldn't let himself go.

Sam had never put himself in those pictures except to wonder, as anyone might, what would I do?

Those terrifying events had been for other people, Sam had always thought. Jewish people, and Sam didn't think of himself as Jewish, not the way his father was. What this book made very clear, however, was that the Nazis were bent on getting rid of anyone who had any Jewish blood in them. They measured it down to the third degree — having a great-grandparent who was Jewish. During Hitler's reign, Sam would have been considered as Jewish as Avi. And they would have come for him, too.

Sam threw the book across the room, hitting his dresser. It packed such a wallop, the bobble-head baseball players on top practically shook their heads off. Fearing that he had awakened someone, he listened intently to the house sounds, but no one seemed to be moving around. If he hadn't been in the mood to talk to God before, he certainly had a few questions for Him now.

"So I would have gone, too?" he said aloud. "Thanks a lot," he added bitterly. He knew it wasn't right to be so angry just because he now realized it could have been him. After all, he knew that kids his own age, like Anne Frank, had spent years in hiding and were discovered, anyway. He knew that children had been separated from their parents, some sent away for their own safety and others simply lost in the fog of war. And, of course, there was no escaping the hideous truth that more than a million children had suffered the final horrible fate. Suddenly, though, it was personal, and tears of anger welled in his eyes.

"Sam?"

He hadn't even realized Ellen was standing in the doorway.

"What's wrong?" she asked with concern.

"Nothing," he answered curtly. Go away, he thought.

Ellen slipped into the room and closed the door behind her. "You're never up this early."

"Neither are you," Sam pointed out. "Why don't you go back to bed?"

"The attic is so drafty. I don't know why I never noticed it. Too happy to have my own space, I guess. I woke up and it was cold, and I thought I heard something down here." She followed Sam's glance to the book that was lying across the room and padded over to it and picked it up. "For your Holocaust unit?" she asked, reading the title.

"Yes. Do you know what the title means?"

Ellen nodded.

"How do you know everything?" Sam burst out. "Why doesn't anyone tell me anything?"

"Sam, I'm in college, you're in junior high. I would hope I know a few more things than you." She put the book on the dresser. "Besides, you're finding out now."

"I wish I weren't," he said, turning over and burying his head in the pillow, so if his tears overflowed, his sister wouldn't see them.

Ellen came over and sat on the edge of the bed and rubbed his back, like she used to do when he was little and had a stomachache. It made him feel like a baby, but he didn't care. It was comforting. "It was a long time ago, Sam."

He rolled over. "Yeah, but it's not like terrible things aren't happening right now. People are always beating up on one another. And one of the things that makes them hate one another is when they're different religions."

"You're right," Ellen said simply.

"So how come God doesn't come down and fix that, if He's so powerful?"

"I don't think it's up to God to fix things."

"Yeah?" Sam said belligerently. "Then who's supposed to fix them?"

Ellen thought about it. "Well, us, I guess."

Sam sat up. "Us? Oh, *us*?" he repeated sarcastically. "How can we do anything about people killing other people in countries a million miles away?"

"It doesn't start with killing," Ellen replied calmly. "First, people don't like one another because they're different. Then they blame one another. Hate one another. And then, sometimes, they kill one another."

Anger colored Sam's face. "Yeah. So what am I supposed to do about that?"

"There *is* something you can do. There's a pretty good rule to follow."

"Which rule is that?"

"The Golden Rule. You know it. 'Do unto others as you would have them do unto you.' In Judaism, it's 'Do not do that which you would not have done to you.' I think that's even more powerful."

Sam considered Ellen's words. "So you just treat people the way you would want to be treated."

"Think of how many problems that would solve," his sister said.

"And the Jewish way?" Sam asked.

"Don't push things on people. Don't make them do things they don't want to do or say. Don't embarrass them. It's not rocket science," she continued. "Pretty easy, really."

"If it's so easy, why doesn't everyone just do it?"

Ellen laughed. "Okay, so it's not all that easy. Not all the time, anyway. But we can keep trying."

Sam and Ellen sat quietly together for several moments. He was surprised to find he felt better. "I miss you, El," he said shyly.

"You couldn't wait for me to go to college."

"That's when I thought I was going to get your room."

They smiled at each other.

"Hey, I can hear you talking," Maxie said, coming into the room.

Ellen pulled him onto her lap, making Sam's bed awfully crowded, but in a good way. "Sorry."

Squirming, he asked, "What's going on, anyway?"

"We were just talking," Sam said.

"It's hardly light outside," Maxie noted.

"I know," Ellen said. "Isn't this fun?"

Maxie nodded. "But what do we do now? We can't just stay in Sam's bed all morning."

"Let's do something nice for Mom and Dad," Ellen suggested. "Why don't we make them breakfast in bed?"

"Okay," Maxie said, sliding off his sister's lap.

Sam found that he was suddenly ravenous. "Yeah, and let's make something for us, too."

Although the Goodman children tried to keep quiet, they were giggling and whispering so loudly, it was a wonder their parents didn't wake up. Actually, Sam was pretty sure they were awake but had figured out what was going on and were waiting for the surprise.

Ellen decided they shouldn't attempt anything too complicated. She made coffee, and together the boys made cinnamon rolls from a tube in the refrigerator, getting more frosting in their mouths than on the rolls. There was an old white wicker tray that Mrs. Goodman used to bring food upstairs when they were sick. Ellen dug it out of the pantry, and Maxie nabbed a fake flower from an arrangement on the dining room table and stuck it in a bud vase. They all grabbed different things — food, mugs and plates, napkins — and brought them upstairs, arranging everything on the tray before they knocked on their parents' door.

Mr. and Mrs. Goodman *ohhed* and *ahhed,* and thanked the children profusely. If Sam's bed was too small for his brother and sister, their parents' king-size bed was — almost — big enough for everyone. Ellen perched on the bed for a few moments, then moved over to the chair from her mother's vanity. Sam, feeling a little self-conscious, scooted down to the very edge of the mattress. But Maxie made himself comfortable and wiggled between his parents.

"This is delicious," Mrs. Goodman complimented them.

"But the rolls are maybe just a little light on the white stuff." Mr. Goodman smiled, wiping some excess frosting from Maxie's upper lip.

The family spent the next half hour or so lounging around and being silly. Maxie had just finished reading a riddle book, so he was full of jokes that he considered hysterical. When he asked, "Why did the pig cross the road on a hot day?" Everyone cried out in unison, "Because he was bakin'!" They had heard it several times before.

Ellen willingly went downstairs several more times to get what Mr. Goodman described as "the most delicious coffee ever made by one of his children," and Sam braved the freezing cold to grab the Sunday newspaper off the mat so everyone could take his or her favorite part and strew it across the bed. Once or twice, the memory of his conversation with Ellen inched along the outskirts of his mind, but Sam moved it away and tried to bask in what used to be a typical family scene. Naturally, it didn't last forever.

Mrs. Goodman leaned over to pick up her watch off the end table and said, "Gee guys, it's getting late. I have to get ready for church."

Although he didn't say anything, Mr. Goodman's expression spoke loudly: Do you have to go?

Annie Goodman answered the unspoken question by saying, "My mother is looking forward to going to St. James, downtown. I don't want to disappoint her." She turned to Sam, "And you were going, too, weren't you?"

The last thing Sam wanted to do was go to church; he wasn't feeling very religious. But he knew his mother would like it if he did, he had said he would, and he still needed to talk to his grandmother. Grimly he got off the bed and said, "I'll get dressed."

Looking at Sam, Ellen said, "I guess I'll come with you."

"You will?" Mrs. Goodman was delighted. "Shall we all go?"

The silence coming from Mr. Goodman's side of the bed felt as if it had shape — large and heavy. He gave her an almost pleading look. "I can't, Annie," and then added, "I have to go see my mother."

"You could go this afternoon," his wife answered quietly.

"She's got a concert she's going to this afternoon. I said I'd drop her off on my way back home."

"All right. What about you, Maxie?"

Sam could see that it was Maxie's turn to be stuck in the middle.

"I didn't see Grandma Sally last week," he said, his eyes darting between his mother and his father.

"I'm sure she wouldn't mind if you went with your mother," Mr. Goodman said.

Maxie thought about the morning as if he were trying to figure out the right answer to a math question. Mrs. Goodman couldn't bear to see him trying to decide. "Look, darling, you go with Daddy like you planned. It's very cold out and we might have a long walk from the parking lot. You can come with me and Nana when it gets warmer."

"All right," Maxie said, relieved.

Mr. Goodman gave his wife a kiss, and everyone felt as

though a balloon had been popped. "Maybe I'll come with you, too, when it gets warmer," he said.

Ellen and Sam exchanged looks. Their father going to church? That would be a first.

Looking as though she didn't quite believe him, Mrs. Goodman smiled, anyway, and kissed him back. "If you want to, David, that would be great."

Sam always enjoyed going into the heart of Chicago. Just catching sight of the skyscrapers as they drove along Lake Michigan made him feel like a big-city kid. He and his mother and sister were meeting Nana at St. James Cathedral, off Michigan Avenue, Chicago's glitziest shopping area. St. James was larger and much more impressive than his mother's church in Evanston. As they entered the large stone building, Sam was taken by the high, high arched ceiling, the handsomely decorated walls, and the many stained-glass windows through which the winter sun was streaming. The church was very full, but the Goodmans found Nana in a pew off to the side, and Sam followed his mother and sister's lead, genuflecting in the aisle before moving into the pew to take a seat. Kissing his grandmother, he picked up a prayer book and listened to the organ playing while he waited for the service to begin.

Sam leafed through the prayer book without really reading it. Closing it, he looked around. The church was restful, he decided. Despite the fact that it was packed, the sanctuary basked in a reverential hush that made it seem as if something important was about to happen. Behind the altar hung a large crucifix, dwarfing everything else. Sam's meager churchgoing had been mostly confined to the church in Evanston, a more modern building than this one, which as far as he could see would not have looked out of place in the Middle Ages. The Evanston church's crucifix was bright and gleaming, but this one, worn and rugged, had more character. It reminded you that someone had died on a cross like this. Sam shivered a little as he thought of it, even though the church was quite warm.

"You okay?" asked Ellen, who was sitting next to him.

"Sure." His eyes refocused on the cross. He knew that Jesus had died for his sins, but he wasn't really sure what that meant. Did he have that many sins? He supposed he had some. Were they enough for someone to die for?

The priest, an older man with long white hair, looking as though he might have stepped out of the Bible himself, walked to the front of the altar and began the service. Unfamiliar with the liturgy, or even the hymns, Sam simply let himself go along with the rhythm of the service, rising when he was supposed to, and obediently sitting down. Here, in church, might have been an excellent place to talk to God, but Sam found it was a relief not to be thinking about anything in particular, to simply let himself float on the music and the words.

When the priest started giving his sermon, though, Sam began to listen. In part, it was because of the priest's voice, which had a slight British accent, making everything he said sound important, but there was also a warmth to it that seemed to wrap itself around Sam like a woollen cloak.

The sermon was about evil in the world. Sam sat up straight. Wasn't that just what he had been asking God about?

"So many bad things happen." The priest stopped and looked around the congregation. "Perhaps 'bad' is not a strong enough word. 'Evil.' That is a word, metallic on the tongue, which rings full with the intention of causing pain and hardship. Evil is in the world, and how is it to be stopped, except by the one force that is more potent? That force is love. Jesus Christ taught 'God is love.' Love, not just for family and friends, but for the stranger, and even for those who cause us grief or even harm. Christ gave us one message above all, to love one another. If we did that one thing — not always simple, but always necessary — how different would our world be?"

Sam thought about that. How different *would* things be? Very, he concluded. The Holocaust had been possible because of the hatred people had felt toward the Jews. Hatred for not much reason, at least as far as Sam could see. All of the fighting that was going on today, too, could be traced back to people refusing to see that those they were angry at were more like them than they were different. Asking people to love their enemies, well, Sam could see that was hard. But starting with the Golden Rule, like Ellen said, and not doing stuff to people that you wouldn't want done to you, well, that shouldn't be so difficult. Should it?

When the sermon was over, it was time for the congregation to take communion. His mother and grandmother rose, and Sam wasn't sure what he was supposed to do. Mrs. Goodman leaned over and whispered, "Don't worry about it, Sam. You don't have to."

Sam nodded with relief. The priest had just said sharing communion meant partaking in the blood and body of Christ. That made him feel uncomfortable, but as he watched most of the people in the church take a wafer in their mouths and sip wine, it didn't look too strange.

"Have you ever done it?" Sam asked.

Ellen shook her head.

After communion, there was one more prayer: "Send us now into the world in peace, and grant us strength and courage to love and serve You with gladness and singleness of heart." Sam stood a little taller as the priest spoke the words.

They went out into the cold, windless day, and Mrs. Goodman said to Nana, "Do you want to go somewhere for lunch?"

"I thought we could do a little shopping before lunch," Ellen interrupted.

"You're always in the mood for shopping," Mrs. Goodman noted dryly.

"That's all right," Nana said. "I want to do a little shopping, too. Why don't we meet in an hour at the Drake, and I'll treat everyone to a lovely lunch."

Mrs. Goodman pulled her hat down around her ears. "Fine. Sam, you go with Nana and you can talk about your project."

Shopping, Sam thought, always with the shopping, but he didn't see any way out of it.

Nana must have read his mind, because she said, "I don't think you'll mind this shopping expedition."

She was right, because instead of going to one of the big department stores that dotted Michigan Avenue, she marched quickly against the cold to a nearby side street where there was a comfy-looking shop devoted to golf and fishing gear. The inside of the cathedral may have been an awe-inspiring dark, rich mahogany, but this store was outfitted in a friendly knotty pine.

"I'm looking for a new reel," she informed Sam as they bustled inside to where it was warm.

"Are you going to take me fishing this summer?" he asked.

"Don't I always? Maybe we'll go up to Lake Geneva for a couple of days. What would you think of that?"

Sam knew that going on a fishing trip with one's grandmother might have sounded weird to a lot of kids his age, but it sounded pretty good to him.

Nana brushed away the salesman who asked her if she needed help. "If I do, I'll let you know," she replied. "I was fishing before that boy's mother was born," she added tartly once he was out of earshot. "I'm the one who should be a salesperson here."

As she picked up a rod and reel, weighing it in her hand, Nana said to him, "So what is this you need to know about World War II?"

Sam leaned against a pillar watching his grandmother handle the rod. "The Holocaust, really," Sam said.

Nana looked up and eyed him sharply. "They make you study that?"

Sam nodded.

"Good," she said emphatically.

That surprised him. He had suspected that his grandmother might have thought that he was too young for the subject. "I'm supposed to talk to people who were alive then and ask them what they remember."

Nana put down the fishing equipment. "I'll never forget a day in nineteen forty-five. I was down at Huber's Drugs and I bought a *Life* magazine to read while I had a cherry soda. I settled in at the soda fountain, leafing through the magazine, and I came across the first photographs showing the liberation of the camps. I was sick to my stomach." Nana shook her head at the memory. "Those poor emaciated souls who had suffered so much because of Hitler's madness."

Sam gave a small sigh of relief. He hadn't realized until that moment how scared he had been that his grandmother might not have seen the Holocaust to be as horrible as it was. He wondered if he could broach the subject with Nana delicately.

"I thought, well, I wasn't sure —" Sam was fumbling.

"What are you trying to say, Sam?"

"Well, it's just that most of the people in the camps were Jewish."

Nana looked bewildered for a few seconds, then her expression darkened. "What are you implying? That I in some way condoned what happened?"

"No, no," an embarrassed Sam backtracked, "but I know you don't get along with Grandma Sally, and Dad, even. . . ."

Sam was afraid Nana was going to blow her top. He had

never seen her look so angry. But then her face cleared, and she pulled him over to a leather couch conveniently placed for those not interested in fishing to rest while their friends or family shopped.

"Sam, it is not true that I don't get along with your father. I think he's a fine man, and I've always respected him. Your other grandmother" — Nana hesitated — "well, it's true we rub each other the wrong way, but I think that might be true even if we sat next to each other at church every Sunday. That doesn't mean I harbor any ill feelings against her."

Sam fell all over himself trying to apologize. "Nana, I never meant —"

Nana's expression softened. "I know. But you're aware that Sally and I have been having a tug-of-war over you children." She shook her head. "That wasn't right. I owe you an apology."

"It's just that I've been reading about all this stuff, about people hating the Jews —"

"Sam, I've never had a problem with Judaism. I have a problem with you being raised without a religion."

"You mean not being raised as an Episcopalian," Sam challenged her.

Nana sighed. "Well, I suppose that's the truth. That *is* important to me. I *have* wanted all you children to be raised in a family where everyone believes the same thing. Where you could have a Christmas tree — not a Christmas tree called a Hanukkah bush as a compromise. And if I'm being honest, which I like to be, I'd prefer that the religion your family follows would be mine. But you aren't being raised that way, and I have to say I've never known three lovelier children." She paused. "So your parents have obviously done plenty right."

Sam smiled with relief as Nana looked at her watch. "We have to be at the Drake soon. I'm afraid I haven't answered many questions about the Holocaust, though."

"Did you know it was happening while it was going on?"

"I guess I knew some of it. Not all of it. We all knew enough, though. We should have known enough to prevent it. I have always imagined that had I been in a position to do something, to harbor someone, or help them escape, I would have done so." With a faraway look on her face, Nana looked into the past. "But can I be sure of that? I don't know. I hope so." She focused back on Sam. "The best we can do is live our lives in a way that makes us believe the answer would be yes."

CHAPTER FIFTEEN

The following Saturday, Sam stood at the living room window waiting for Avi's father to pick him up. He was a little nervous about having to make conversation with him for who-knew-how-long as they waited for Avi to finish up at the synagogue, but Mr. Cohen was his only way to the mall. Sam's mother was spending her Saturday at a teachers' conference, and his dad had to be in the office for a breakfast meeting with his partners. Maxie had already been dropped off at Nana's.

"But how am I going to get to the mall?" Sam had asked indignantly when the weekend's plans were shaping up.

"Sam," his mother had asked with a sigh, "would the world fall apart if you missed one Saturday?"

Yes! Sam wanted to shout. Yes, it would! Because the mall was the one place where he and Heather could hang out together and act like they were boyfriend and girlfriend. Sam walked Heather to class when he could and they instant messaged, though they were rarely online at the same time. But only on the few Saturdays that they had had together since

Vicki's party did Sam really feel like Heather and he were a couple. They didn't do much: just goofed around, or went to the movies with a bunch of other people. There had been no more parties and no more kisses; Sam had managed to hold Heather's hand in the movies, but his palm was so sweaty, he constantly wanted to pull away and wipe it on his pants.

Although Sam would have been loath to admit it, time spent with Heather was equal parts trepidation and exhilaration. He couldn't say that he felt comfortable with Heather yet. She seemed to like keeping Sam off balance — there was no relaxing when he was around her. Only a few days ago he'd been talking to Will at his locker when Heather had interrupted to tell Sam she was going to pick up her new kitten after school. Her eyes were sparkling, and she grabbed his hand with excitement. Sam had wanted to lean over and kiss her right in the middle of the crowded hallway. Instead, leaving a smirking Will behind, he walked Heather outside as she chattered about the white angora cat. She'd asked Sam to come over that evening but when he replied he didn't think so (how would he choke out the words, "Dad, can you take me over to Heather's so I can see her cat?"), she had turned on him. Her blue eyes grew stormy, and she looked like she was going to stamp her foot. Sam had apologized profusely; only when he was sure that she had forgiven him did he feel a welcome rush of relief. As unnerving as that sort of tension was, being with Heather also gave Sam a jolt that made him feel as if he had drunk one Coca-Cola too many. Was he really up to Heather Daniels? Sam sometimes wondered. Then he would remind himself that she had chosen him. That said something about Sam Goodman, didn't it?

When it became clear that the Goodman chauffeur service was not going to be in business this Saturday, Sam knew he was going to have to be creative in finding alternative means of transportation. After several phone calls to Avi, they arranged for Mr. Cohen to do their hauling. Avi had to go to his regular bar mitzvah preparation class, but Mr. Cohen agreed to pick Sam up before he picked up Avi, and then he would drop them off at the mall. By the time they were ready to go home, Mr. Goodman would be able to pick them up. Sam looked at his watch and then glanced nervously out the window. He hoped Mr. Cohen hadn't forgotten about him. In just a few minutes, however, Mr. Cohen pulled into the driveway, and Sam hurried outside before he could honk.

"Hi, Sam, how are you doing?" Mr. Cohen greeted him.

"Okay."

The silence Sam had been dreading descended on the car. Sam tried frantically to think of something to say, with no success. Thankfully, Mr. Cohen started asking him about school. They talked about going out for the baseball team, and if Sam was going to take Spanish next year so he could get some language in before high school. Then they started talking about Avi's bar mitzvah.

"I know he's nervous," Mr. Cohen said, "but he's going to be great. His Hebrew is flawless," he added proudly.

"I've been to a couple of bar mitzvahs," Sam said, "but never one for anybody I knew very well."

"It's a wonderful ceremony. Bar mitzvahs for the boys, bat mitzvahs for the girls; I always feel proud when I see kids up there reading in Hebrew, taking their places in the Jewish community. It's going to be even more exciting when the boy is mine."

"So you like being Jewish?" Sam couldn't believe he'd said that. Where had that question come from?

Mr. Cohen turned and smiled at him. "It's a perfect religion for me. I like feeling a part of something that's been around for five thousand years. I like the holidays and the way the year revolves around them, and I especially like the way Judaism makes people take responsibility for their own actions."

"It does?" Sam wasn't exactly sure what Mr. Cohen meant by that.

"Oh yes, Judaism lays out very specific ways people have to be responsible for what they have done. I'm sure you've heard of Yom Kippur, the Day of Atonement?"

Sam nodded. His grandmother always went to synagogue on that day, and she spent it fasting.

"Well, on Yom Kippur, you ask God to forgive the sins you've committed during the past year. But He can only forgive the sins you've committed against Him. For sins committed against another person, you must go to him or her and ask for their forgiveness."

Sam thought that sounded a little scary. "I guess that makes you think about what you've done," he said tentatively.

"Sure does."

Well, he was into it now, Sam thought. He might as well continue the conversation. "But isn't it hard to be Jewish? I mean, lots of terrible things have happened to the Jews."

Mr. Cohen paused. "Yes, but look, we're still here after all of it. I suppose you're thinking about the Holocaust in particular. Avi says you're almost finished with your unit. What do you have left to do?"

"Just write a paper about what I've learned. No test. Mr. Tibold said reducing the Holocaust to a list of questions and answers would be insulting to the memory of those who died."

"A wise decision," Mr. Cohen said. "So what did you learn? If you don't mind my asking."

Sam appreciated Mr. Cohen respecting his privacy, but he was okay with answering. "I learned lots of stuff about why it happened, but I still can't believe that people did that to other people," Sam murmured.

"It is hard to believe, I grant you."

Sam remembered that Mr. Cohen once said he almost became a rabbi. Wouldn't a rabbi be especially angry at God for the Holocaust? Sam wondered. Rabbis, and other religious leaders, too, were supposed to spend their time telling people how great God was. Hadn't the Holocaust made God a hard sell for the rabbis? Sam tried to think of a way to broach the question without sounding too insulting. It wasn't one that he would have dared bring up with his father.

"Uh, Mr. Cohen," he began.

"Yes, Sam?"

"Don't you think, well, isn't it hard for Jews to keep believing in God after the Holocaust? I mean, after everything He let happen to them?" There, he'd asked it.

Mr. Cohen found a parking space in the synagogue parking lot. Avi was nowhere to be seen. He thought about Sam's question, and then he said, "I can't speak for all Jews, Sam. I'm sure some people did lose their faith after the Holocaust. But I don't believe the Holocaust was God's fault. It was the fault of people. *Some* people." Mr. Cohen turned toward Sam. "I don't suppose you know what the Hebrew word *tikkun* means?"

Sam shook his head.

"Well, it means to repair. To repair and restore the world. You see, there's a Jewish idea that says that God made the world with holes in it, and he made people to repair those holes. Events like the Holocaust are big black holes in the world, but it's up to people, ordinary people like you and me, to help mend them." Mr. Cohen smiled at Sam, a little sadly, Sam thought. "Does that make any sense to you at all?"

Sam was almost surprised to find it did make sense. Maybe a couple of months ago it wouldn't have. But today, it did.

"Hey!" Avi was rapping on the door of the car. Neither Sam nor Mr. Cohen had seen him arrive. "Wow," he said as he climbed in the backseat, "it's cold out there."

The contemplative mood in the car was broken. Along with the blast of frigid air, Avi brought his sunny optimism into the car, and today Sam felt warmed by it.

"So what were you two talking about?" Avi asked. "You looked so serious."

Sam and Mr. Cohen exchanged a quick glance.

"We were wondering if you were still going to fit in your bar mitzvah suit," Mr. Cohen said. "You've grown about two inches since we bought it."

"Oh, you were not," Avi said.

Sam realized that Avi's father was right, however. Avi was getting awfully tall awfully fast. He was beginning to tower over Sam.

"So where do you boys want to go?" Mr. Cohen asked teasingly as he started up the car. "A museum, the Art Institute?"

"Let me see," Avi said, pretending to think about it. "Uh, how about the Red Oak Mall?"

Mr. Cohen obligingly headed toward the mall. "There's a surprising choice."

As Sam thanked Mr. Cohen for the ride as he got out of the car, he almost felt as if he should thank him for the conversation as well. It had just been getting started and had been interrupted too soon. Sam thought Mr. Cohen gave him a measured look as he said good-bye, but he couldn't be sure.

As Sam entered Red Oak, he noted that a person could forgo calendars if they made regular visits to the mall; you could tell the time of year by the decorations. It had been presents, Christmas trees, and menorahs in December, giant snowflakes in January, and now hearts and cupids studded the atrium and were artfully placed in store windows. If Sam hadn't known the exact date of Valentine's Day last month, he knew it now. And if he somehow contracted amnesia, he would be reminded by the banners in the card shop and candy store windows: DON'T FORGET YOUR SWEETIE ON FEBRUARY 14.

Sam knew that Heather was expecting some sort of present; picking it out was going to be like stepping his way through a minefield. Here was the agony and ecstasy of going with Heather in one signature experience — agony if he got the wrong thing; ecstasy if he should, by some miracle, get it right.

"Hey, Avi?"

"Hmmm?" Avi was striding past the Gap, past Foot Locker and Pottery Barn toward the food court, scanning the mall walkers for familiar faces.

"Are you getting Vicki something for Valentine's Day?" Vicki and Avi had been almost inseparable since her party, but unlike Sam and Heather, they seemed to feel supremely comfortable together, always laughing and goofing around. Sam didn't know how Avi could possibly act that way around a girl he liked.

Avi kept walking nonchalantly as if Sam had asked him if he was going to buy a new pair of socks. "Sure."

"Do you know what it's going to be?" Sam asked, impressed.

"Sure."

"Well, what?"

Avi looked at Sam as if he were stupid. "A box of chocolates in a red-heart box. Not too personal, not too expensive, and everyone likes chocolate."

Sam thought back to the boxes of candy that he had bought for his grandmothers. Those hadn't been too successful, but perhaps that was due more to circumstances than to the actual chocolates themselves. "Yeah," Sam said, nodding as though Avi had passed on the wisdom of the world. "Chocolates."

"Nobody's here yet," Avi said, skidding to a stop in front of the McDonald's. "At least I don't see anyone."

"I do," Sam said. Off in a corner sat Heather giggling with Britt. Then she looked up, saw Sam, and gave him a little wave. Sam glanced around to see if anyone else was noticing that the prettiest girl in the Red Oak Mall was waving at him. Sadly, it didn't appear that anyone was.

Avi peered in Heather's direction and made a face. "Why don't you go over there? I'll meet you later," he said.

Sam hated that he had found yet another way to be caught in the middle. He would have been perfectly happy to sit with Avi and Vicki; would it be so difficult for Avi to just plunk himself down on a chair in front of the Johnny Rockets? Apparently so, as Sam watched Avi melt into the crowds of people carrying plastic trays and looking for a table. Squaring his shoulders, he hurried over to Heather's table.

"Hi, Sam," Heather and Britt said almost in unison. Then Heather gave Britt a look that Sam hoped he was reading right. It seemed to say, "Get out of here."

Britt made a face. "Um, I'm going to meet Carrie at that new jewelry store. I guess I'll catch up later."

"Bye, bye," Heather said brightly.

"So," Sam began, grappling for a conversational opener as he sometimes did when he was alone with Heather, "what were you guys laughing about?"

"Oh, you saw us? We were just watching the fat people waddle by."

"What?"

"You know" — Heather made an expansive gesture with her hand — "all the fat people that walk around in the mall. Of course, in the winter, you can't really see how fat some of them are because they're wearing coats. But in the summer . . . well, it's like my mother always says, it's unreal how some people let themselves go."

Sam shifted in his seat uncomfortably as Ellen's request to dance with a fat girl flashed into his mind. Thoughts of saying something to Heather about her rude comments arose and then sank just as quickly. He didn't want to start a fight or anything. Better to just change the subject. But before he could come up with a topic, Heather said, "February fourteenth is coming up. . . ."

Sam nodded proudly like the smartest kid in the class. "Valentine's Day."

Heather smiled at him. "So what are we going to do?"

Do? What did she mean *do*? Understanding dawned swiftly. Oh, no; thanks to Avi, he had just gotten the gift issue settled. Now he was expected to come up with an idea for an actual *date*? He looked at Heather, who looked right back at him, expectation written all over her face.

"Well," he began slowly. "Ah, what day of the week is that?"

"Friday," Heather responded promptly.

"Okay, Friday, so we could do something —"

"Friday night."

"Sure. Friday night. We could . . . uh, come to the mall."

Heather frowned.

Sam scrambled. "And go to a movie." There. That was a date, wasn't it?

Heather thought about it for a moment. "Yeah, we could, but there would be so many other kids around."

She didn't want other kids around? She wanted to be alone with him? Where exactly would that be? Sam thought frantically.

Perhaps taking pity on Sam, Heather said, "I have an idea."

"You do?" he said with a mixture of hope and fear.

"Why don't we go ice-skating?"

"Ice-skating," Sam repeated, stalling for time. Well, he supposed that was all right. He used to have a pair of ice skates; perhaps they didn't fit anymore, but he thought you could rent ice skates at the big community rink that was only a few blocks from his home. He could possibly walk there. Then he'd only have to have someone pick him up. Unless, of course, he was supposed to escort Heather to the skating rink. No, she couldn't expect that, could she? Then he'd have to meet her parents. He really didn't feel ready. . . .

"Sam?"

"Oh, sorry, I was just thinking about something. Uh, yeah, ice-skating might be fun."

"I used to take lessons," Heather confided. "I don't anymore. I figured out I was never going to make the Olympics," she said with a laugh that didn't sound entirely natural. "But I still have the costumes, and I still like to skate."

Costumes? A vision of those cute ice-skaters on television wearing those short, swirly skirts flashed in front of Sam's eyes.

"Skating's a great idea," he told Heather sincerely. "I can't wait."

CHAPTER
SIXTEEN

It wasn't hard for Sam to keep his parents in the dark about his Valentine's Day date with Heather. Even though he was pretty sure they wouldn't give him any flack, he didn't want them to make a big deal of it. *He* didn't want to make a big deal of it. So Sam casually dropped the news midweek that he was going ice-skating on Friday night. Details were not offered and thankfully not asked for.

All that his mother said was, "Great. Do your skates still fit you?"

"I'll check," Sam promised.

Finding his skates took a while. They eventually turned up in a cardboard box in the garage. Sitting down on the concrete floor, Sam unlaced a skate and pulled it on. Tight. Pretty darn tight, but they would work. Sam felt relieved — one problem was now taken care of. From what Heather had said, it sounded as if she was practically a professional skater, so rented skates seemed out of the question. The last thing he wanted to do was whirl her around the rink — at least that's how he pictured their skating in his mind — in ugly rented skates.

But with the skates safely off the table, Sam now had time to worry about something else. Oddly, now that he and Heather had made a real date, their relationship had deteriorated. It was hard for Sam to figure out. Heather had seemed so insistent about doing something on Valentine's Day, and now, with that something set up, she was acting as if she barely knew him.

During the few minutes between one of their history and English classes he tried talking to her.

"Heather, about Friday?"

Heather barely looked up from her paper. "Hmmm?"

"Is it okay if we meet at the rink?" He braced himself for the answer. Sam wasn't sure that he was going to be able to go if the answer was no.

"Oh, that's fine," she replied.

"So, is seven thirty okay?"

Heather nodded.

Sam couldn't shake the feeling Heather was mad at him, but couldn't imagine what he had done to raise her ire. Everything had been fine on Saturday. After firming up the ice-skating plans, they had hooked up with a bunch of other kids hanging out at the mall, including some of the eighth graders. A fresh snowfall gave them the idea for a snowball fight, in a small wooded area that was on the far side of one of the parking lots, but as the whole group was heading outside, Sam's cell phone — the one his mother gave him to use on Saturdays — rang in his pocket. Maxie needed a babysitter, and Mrs. Goodman said she had to go out and that she would be by to pick him up immediately. Before she gave him any time to argue, she'd hung up. At the time, Heather seemed sad to see him go; by Monday, she acted like she'd forgotten his name.

"Heather?" Sam said tentatively, clearing his throat.

This time, she did focus her attention on him. "What?"

"Is anything wrong?"

"Wrong?" She shook her head. "No, nothing's wrong."

On Friday evening, after dinner, it began snowing yet again. It had snowed lightly earlier in the day, and the flakes were still just a frosting on the streets, but a bigger storm was predicted for later that night.

Ellen had come home for a follow-up appointment with her dentist. "Do you want me to drive you over to the rink?" she asked as she was loading the dishwasher.

"Oh no, that's fine, I can walk." He glanced over at his mother, who was putting away leftovers, but she didn't seem to be paying any attention to him.

Ellen looked at her brother suspiciously. "Since when do you like to walk anywhere?"

"I can use the exercise," he replied. His answer sounded lame even to his own ears, but Ellen just shrugged. "Whatever you want."

"You'll need a ride home, though, Sam," his mother said. Apparently, she *had* been listening.

"Oh, I won't be late," Sam protested. "The rink closes at ten."

"I don't want you walking home that time of night," Mrs. Goodman said, shaking her head. "Your father and I are going to the movies tonight. But Ellen can get you." She turned to her daughter. "Okay?"

"Sure, I'm just going to be home studying and babysitting Maxie. Should I bring him with me?"

Mrs. Goodman frowned. "That's a little late for him to be up. Maybe you can get a ride with one of the other kids?" she asked Sam.

Sam didn't like lying to his mother, yet as far as he knew, none of his friends were going to be at the rink. "Sure, maybe."

"Well, if you can't get a ride," Mrs. Goodman said, improvising arrangements, "you'll just have to come home by nine. Then Ellen can get you and bring Maxie with her."

"I'll call if I need a ride," Sam said carefully. There, that was the truth, sort of. He felt like he'd better get out of the kitchen quickly before some other sticking point came up, but as he was walking by the refrigerator, he noticed something being held up by a magnet to the door.

"What's this?" he asked his mother as he pulled down the large cream-colored square embellished with a small Jewish star.

"Oh, I meant to show it to you. The invitation to Avi's bar mitzvah came today."

Sam examined the invitation written in a fancy script. It gave the location of the synagogue and said there would be a luncheon in a hotel after the ceremony. Sam knew the lunch was more of a party; that's where the dancing would take place.

"Are we all invited?" Sam asked his mother.

"Yes. Ellen may not be able to make it, but Dad and I and Maxie are going. We won't cramp your style, will we?" she asked, shrewdly guessing what was on Sam's mind.

Sam caught his sister's eye. She made a sympathetic face.

"I guess not," Sam said in a resigned tone.

Mrs. Goodman laughed. "We'll try not to look in your direction."

Sam glanced once more at the invitation before handing it back to his mother. He would turn thirteen at the end of April. Was there going to be anything special to mark that occasion?

By 7:10, Sam had his jacket on and was ready to go. His skates — and a box of Valentine's candy he had purchased at the drugstore — were in his backpack. The goal was to make an exit with a minimum of attention paid to his departure. "Okay, I'm leaving," Sam called.

No one seemed to be around, but his father came out of the family room at the sound of Sam's voice. "Are you sure you don't want a ride?" he asked, looking out the window. "It's still snowing."

"It'll take you longer to clean off the car than it will for me to walk over to the rink," Sam said, trying to get out of the house without looking like he was trying to get out of the house.

"Well, not quite, but walk if you want to." Mr. Goodman's eyes left the window and focused on Sam. It was almost as if he were seeing him for the first time in a long time. "Do you know how tall you're getting?" he said, in a surprised voice. "You're almost as tall as me."

Truth be told, Mr. Goodman wasn't all that tall, but it made Sam feel extremely odd for his father to notice they were nearly the same height. "Yeah, but not yet," he said uncomfortably.

Mr. Goodman stepped forward as if to give his son a hug, but Sam opened the door, easing his way outside. "Bye, Dad. See you later."

Freedom at last. The snow was still coming down lightly, but it was freezing over what had already fallen, giving the sidewalks an icy crunch as Sam walked along. When he got to

Avi's house, Sam noticed his friend in the detached garage, fumbling around for something.

"Hey, what are you doing?" Sam called from the end of the Cohens' driveway.

Avi turned. "Hi. I'm looking for salt, to throw around and melt the ice. Oh, here it is." Avi moved toward Sam, sprinkling salt grains from a big plastic bag in front of him. "I guess you're going skating?"

Avi was the only one with whom Sam had shared the news of his date and had made him promise not to tell anyone else. He wasn't sure why, since he assumed Heather had talked about it with Britt and her other friends, but come to think of it, no one had acted like they knew.

"Yep." Sam checked his glow-in-the-dark watch. He still had plenty of time, and there was something he wanted to ask Avi. "But you know what? Heather doesn't seem all that into it."

Looking up from his salt sprinkling, Avi said, "No?"

Sam shook his head. "And I was thinking, well, did anything happen after I left the mall last Saturday?"

"Last Saturday." The way Avi said it, it might as well have been last year.

"You know," Sam responded a bit impatiently, "when everyone went outside for the snowball fight."

Avi stopped his salting. "Okay, right. Yeah, we started

throwing snowballs, but pretty soon one of the mall guards came over and told us to quit it, so we did." Avi shrugged. "So that was about it."

"And Heather was just in the middle of it like everyone else?"

Considering for a minute, Avi finally said, "I wasn't really paying attention to Heather, but I think I saw Robert Erlich wash her face with snow."

Robert Erlich? The coolest guy in the eighth grade had washed his Heather's face with snow? Even though girls acted as though they hated it when a gloved hand pushed wet clumped snow in their faces, Sam was pretty sure their out-rage was just an act. Their squeals often seemed more excited than exasperated. Sam could just picture Robert laughing with Heather as a mock battle ensued. Then he remembered back to New Year's Eve, standing and watching a confident Robert holding out his hand to a girl at the dance. Suddenly, his uneasiness about Heather had a name. And it was Robert Erlich.

"Sam?" Avi said inquiringly. "What's up?"

"Nothing." This was one thing he didn't feel like sharing. "I guess I'd better get going."

Slipping and sliding on the icy sidewalks, Sam tried to put his worries about the evening out of his mind. He was going to see Heather and it was going to be great, he told himself.

And sure enough, when he arrived at the ice rink, there was Heather, in a big bulky sweater and a short little skirt and tights, just as he'd hoped. She was doing a few twirls on the ice, and when she caught sight of him, she gave him a wave with her mittened hand that seemed friendly enough. "Hello," she said, skating over to him.

"Hi, I guess I'll put my skates on," he said, shrugging off his backpack and flopping down on a bench.

"Go ahead, I'm going to do a few turns around the ice to warm up."

As he struggled to put on and lace up his skates, Sam watched Heather race around the ice and thought that she looked just as good as those skaters he watched on TV. Unfortunately, the realization was also dawning that he should have spent a few more minutes trying on his skates. The tightness he had felt in the garage now seemed like a major scrunch. When he got up to hobble out onto the ice, Sam knew that he looked awkward and felt worse.

Yet, Heather didn't seem to mind. She seemed so happy to be skating that she just took his gloved hand and pulled him out onto the ice. The rink was well lit, and there were several older teenagers out and one family also skating; but even with these intruders, Sam was able to pretend that he and Heather were by themselves, the snow swaying around them. Hand in hand, they kept circling the ice until Sam could no longer ignore the fact that his toes felt as if they were being crushed in a vise. He endured it for as long as he could, and then even longer, just so he didn't have to ruin Heather's good time, but finally he murmured, "Can we sit down for a few minutes?"

"Already?" she responded with disappointment. "You're not too bad a skater."

Sam ignored the faint praise. "It's just that my skates are a little tight. I haven't worn them in a while."

Heather sighed. "All right, why don't you watch me while I practice some spins."

Rubbing his arms to keep himself warm, Sam sat on a bench and watched Heather do some moves he recognized from the skaters on television — perhaps not as well executed, but recognizable just the same. Then, his eyes strayed to a couple of new figures on the ice. Leaning forward, Sam watched as one of them skated up to Heather. Was it? Yes, it was, Robert Erlich.

Now what was he supposed to do? Robert and Heather were just skating together slowly and talking, but Sam felt foolish. Should he join them? Or just sit on his cold, hard bench and watch?

Heather started skating toward him, leaving Robert to go back to his friends. Maybe the meeting had been accidental after all and not planned as he suspected.

"How are you doing?" Heather asked solicitously. She seemed in a much better mood.

Sam grabbed for the railing and stood up. "I'm fine. Let's go back out."

Heather shook her head. "I'm ready for a rest. Why don't we go inside and get some hot chocolate?"

That surprised Sam, but at least he was prepared for this contingency, having opened his piggy bank and brought along twenty dollars for snacks and whatever else Heather might want.

After changing into their street shoes, they went into the café that adjoined the rink and picked up a couple of hot chocolates, piled high with whipped cream.

"So who were you talking to out there?" Sam said casually when they got settled.

"Huh? Oh, Robert Erlich. You know him, don't you?"

"I've seen him around," Sam said curtly.

"He's going to try out for the hockey team when he gets to high school," Heather informed Sam.

How did she know that? he thought.

"He's very good," she continued.

Sure, much better than Sam "not-too-bad" Goodman in his sixth-grade skates. Sam thought he'd better change the subject. "Did you get the invitation to Avi's bar mitzvah today?"

She took a long swig of her hot chocolate. "Yes."

"I think it will be fun," he said to Heather, who was looking decidedly underwhelmed.

"We don't have to go to the service part, do we?" she asked.

"What do you mean?"

"Well, the lunch sounds okay, but I don't want to sit through a long, boring service watching Avi Cohen yap in a language nobody understands."

"It's Hebrew."

"Like I said." Heather shrugged.

"They speak Hebrew in Israel," Sam said quietly.

Heather seemed to miss the point. "And that's another reason I don't want to go to the bar mitzvah. I'm so tired of reading and hearing about the Jews."

Sam almost choked on his hot chocolate. "Excuse me?"

Heather gave an unconcerned wave of the hand. "Well, haven't you had it with all that Holocaust stuff? My parents say they shouldn't even be subjecting us to it. Too gruesome. Besides, it all happened about a million years ago. Why can't the Jews just get over it?"

Sam felt as if the room were shifting and turning, making him feel slightly queasy. What should he say in answer to that? Should he ignore the comment, or call Heather on it? She seemed to be waiting for an answer, so Sam finally managed,

"Something that bad is pretty hard to forget, Heather." It sounded wishy-washy even to his own ears.

"It's not that I don't feel sorry for them," Heather said, putting down her mug, "and the Nazis didn't have the right to just start killing people, but the Jews should have figured out they weren't wanted in Germany and gotten out."

"Those Jews were Germans," Sam said, some heat finally coloring his voice. "Everywhere the Nazis moved, Poland, France, Holland, they rounded up people who were citizens — like everyone else. They just had a different religion. And in most cases, they didn't have anywhere else to go."

Heather shrugged. "Like my mother always says, people should stick with their own kind. It solves a lot of problems. I don't think the Jews ever got that."

The room straightened itself, and Sam's voice grew strong and sharp. "Heather, I'm Jewish."

Now, finally, Sam had Heather's attention. "You're Jewish?" she repeated dumbly.

"My father is Jewish, my grandmother is Jewish, and in Nazi Germany that would have made me just as Jewish as them. Or any of the people they murdered." He waited for her to say something, but for once, she was as tongue-tied as he usually was. Finally, she muttered, "You should have said something earlier."

"Why, would that have changed what you were thinking?"

Before she could reply, if she had any intention to, he charged on. "What's wrong with you? Dissing Jews and fat people, and Hank Chin. Double whammy on him, huh, Heather? Chinese *and* a dork."

Anger propelled him upward. He looked down at Heather. With her unblinking eyes and spots of color flushing her cheeks, she looked more like a marionette than the girl he had been so enamored with.

Heather finally found her voice. "Sam, sit down," she hissed. "You're making a scene," she told him, even though there was no one in the café. For some reason, her words only emboldened Sam.

"I'm not sitting down. I'm leaving." He checked the big picture window that looked out over the rink. "Robert's still out there. You were probably waiting for him, anyway." As he grabbed his backpack, Sam remembered that Heather's Valentine's chocolates were inside. For an instant he thought about dramatically flinging the box down on the table and saying sarcastically, "Happy Valentine's Day." Then he decided, what the heck, he would just eat the candy himself.

Walking home, Sam was barely aware how bitter the cold had become. The snow that was falling now seemed more like tiny pellets of ice, but his many emotions that were swirling faster than the snow took all of his attention. Alternately, Sam was mad, sad, disappointed, and disgusted, the latter, mostly at himself. Scratch the surface and it had been plain all along that Heather wasn't a nice person. Except for her looks, there was nothing to recommend her, nada, zip.

Ready to be honest with himself, Sam had to admit Heather's seventh-grade snobbery wasn't a shock; he had made an effort to ignore all the evidence in front of him: everything from Avi's opinion of Heather to the way she made fun of people when it suited her purposes. True, kids dumped on other kids all the time, but they seemed like amateurs compared with Heather. People suffering and dying? Hey, it was nothing to her. Something Mr. Tibold had quoted during one of his classes kept gnawing at Sam, but he couldn't quite remember the words. Then it came to him: "All it takes for evil to flourish is for good men to do nothing." Heather wasn't evil, and he wasn't all that good, Sam realized that, but he felt that tonight somehow he had struck a small blow for right. If nothing else, he had taken a stand.

Whether it was his mood or just a desire to get out of the miserable weather, Sam walked so quickly, he was in front of his house before he realized it. Barreling inside, he was wiping off his shoes when Ellen and Maxie appeared in front of him, both of them looking shaken to the core.

"Thank goodness, you're home," Ellen said, her voice quavering. "Mom and Dad were in a car accident."

CHAPTER SEVENTEEN

"A car accident?" Sam was barely able to get the words out. "What happened?"

"Mom called a little while ago from the hospital —"

"So she's all right?" Sam interrupted.

Ellen nodded. "She's okay."

"But Dad . . . ?"

"They just took him into surgery." Ellen put her arms around Maxie, who looked scared to death. "They're not sure what's wrong with him, but he was unconscious, and bleeding."

Sam didn't know what to say, to think, or to feel. "What happened?" he repeated.

"They left for the movies right after you did. They hit a patch of ice, the car spun into the other lane, and they got hit by an oncoming car." Ellen spoke in an almost robotic voice, as if she were just reciting a set of meaningless words.

"What should we do?"

"I'm going to the hospital. Mom didn't want me to drive, so she called Mr. Cohen, and he's going to pick me up any minute."

It just registered with Sam that Ellen was wearing her coat.

"You stay here with Maxie."

"Absolutely not," Sam said, shaking his head. "I'm coming with you."

"That's what I said, I want to come, too," Maxie pleaded, near tears.

"Maxie should stay here," Sam agreed, "but I'm going."

"Then I'm going," Maxie insisted.

Mr. Cohen's car pulled into their driveway.

"He's here," Ellen said, looking distracted. "All right, Maxie, put on your coat. I don't even know if you're too young to be in the hospital, but we don't have time to argue about it."

While Ellen bustled Maxie into his jacket, Sam, grim-faced, went out to the car and got in alongside Mr. Cohen.

"How are you doing, kiddo?" Mr. Cohen asked.

Sam just shrugged. He didn't feel like talking.

The car was silent as they went the short few miles to the hospital.

"Evanston Hospital has lots of fine doctors," Mr. Cohen said, "I'm sure your father will have wonderful care there."

Strange thoughts flew through Sam's mind. He was almost as tall as his father, but he wasn't sure how tall his dad was. Five eight? Five nine? Maybe when he was recuperating in the hospital, they could measure him. Sam wished he had hugged his father when he'd left this evening, but why would he have done that? Hugging wasn't something you did when you left the house on an ordinary night. Of course, this wasn't an ordinary night. No, this night had turned out quite differently from the way he'd expected, but how could he have known? Maybe if he'd stayed home, not gone chasing after Heather, he could have persuaded his parents not to go out tonight, but that was silly, why would they have cancelled the movies just because —

"We're here," Mr. Cohen said as they pulled into the indoor parking lot. They took an elevator to the reception area, and then let Mr. Cohen figure out where they should go. He hustled them up an escalator and down a hall, until they came to a spacious waiting room, where Mrs. Goodman was sitting by herself, looking very small and very alone. She was just staring at a double door, clearly waiting for someone, but Sam wasn't sure if it was a doctor she was looking for or if she somehow expected his father to come strolling out.

Ellen and Maxie ran up to her and threw themselves into her

arms, waking her out of her reverie, but Sam held back. He didn't want her to see how scared he was. But she looked up over the heads of Ellen and Maxie and motioned him toward her, and he, too, got swept up in the family embrace.

Maxie spoke first. "I had to come, Mommy."

"That's all right, my baby," Mrs. Goodman replied as the children pushed back and gave her space to breathe. "I'm glad you're all here. Strength in numbers." She got up and went over to Mr. Cohen, grabbed his hand, and said, "Thanks for bringing the children, Michael."

"Have you heard anything?"

"He's been in surgery for about a half hour. I don't know how long he's going to be in there. They're trying to find out the source of the bleeding."

A tiny, gray-haired African-American woman wearing a blue smock bustled over to them. "Your family, Mrs. Goodman?" she asked.

"Yes. Ellen, Sam, Maxie, this is Mrs. Winters, she's a volunteer here and she's been keeping me company." Mrs. Goodman smiled at her tremulously.

"Can I get you children anything to drink?" Mrs. Winters asked.

The three young Goodmans mutely shook their heads. Sam felt as though he might never eat or drink anything again.

Mrs. Winters gave Ellen a kindly pat. "I told your mother

where to find everything, the coffee machines, the rest rooms, the chapel —"

Mrs. Goodman looked up. "I think I would like to go to the chapel now."

"Me too," Ellen said softly.

"Why don't we all go?" suggested Mr. Cohen.

Mrs. Winters pointed them in the right direction, and Mrs. Goodman, holding tightly to Maxie's hand and trailed by Sam, Ellen, and Mr. Cohen, went into the dimly lit chapel. As they slid into the wood pews, Sam looked around. The room was restful, but almost bare, with only pots of flowers at the front of the chapel for decoration. Then he noticed the small, silvery stars painted on the deep blue ceiling; they reminded him of the time he and his father had taken a camping trip, sleeping under a sky so dark, you could see the millions of stars dotting it in a way that was impossible in the city.

Sam watched his mother kneeling, her head bowed in prayer, while Ellen sat with her eyes closed, and Maxie leaned against her looking as if he was crying more than praying. Mr. Cohen's hands were folded in his lap as he, too, looked up at the silver stars.

They were all communicating with God in their own ways, Sam knew. Now that Sam had talked to God, he knew what to expect when he started a conversation. He had to admit he usually began in a belligerent tone: Why did You do this? Why did You let that happen? He always wondered if God heard him. But tonight it occurred to Sam that perhaps the soft quiet that enveloped him afterward was the sound of God listening. Sam wasn't sure. It was clear God wasn't going to answer him in a big thundering voice the way he had expected at first. Maybe God's answers came quietly, in the voices of other people: his parents, his grandmothers, the priest at St. James, Mr. Cohen, even Ellen, Avi, and Maxie. Every one of them had helped, in small and large ways, to answer his questions.

Now, he asked God to help his father. "Please, please, please," he repeated silently over and over. God didn't need him to be more specific than that, he knew. He just kept saying, "Please," and finally he felt a gentleness inside of him take the edge off of the fear.

When everyone came back into the waiting room, a startling sight awaited them. There, sitting together on one of the couches, was Nana with her arm around Grandma Sally, who looked as if she had been crying.

Mrs. Goodman hurried over to them. "Mom, I told you not to come. And Sally, how did you get here?"

Both grandmothers protested. "I was not going to sit by my phone while you were here worrying," Nana said emphatically.

"You think I could stay home while David was in surgery?" Grandma Sally asked. "I called a cab as soon as I hung up with you."

"Could you have stayed home if it were one of your children, Ann?" Nana added, backing up Grandma Sally.

Mrs. Goodman gave them each a kiss. "I should have known you'd be here. I just didn't want you coming out in such horrible weather. I was just trying to keep you safe."

Grandma Sally gestured over to Mrs. Winters. "That nice lady over there said no word yet."

Mrs. Goodman shook her head. "No word."

"What about the person in the other car?" Nana wanted to know.

"His air bag saved him, thank goodness. But the front of his car crashed into David's door." Annie Goodman sat down next to Nana and put her head on her mother's shoulder, and Nana stroked her hair.

"I'm sure David is going to be just fine!" Nana stated emphatically.

Sam immediately felt better, and the rest of his family seemed to perk up, too. There was something so resolute and confident about Nana's declaration that it seemed as if Mr. Goodman would hear it in the operating room, and know that he had no option other than to get well.

"From your mouth to God's ears, Jane," Grandma Sally answered her with a weak smile.

After what seemed like an eternity of leafing through a magazine without looking at it, Sam threw it down on the

246

end table from which he had picked it up. He wished someone would come and tell them something; the waiting was
unendurable. Maxie was stretched out on the couch asleep,
but everyone else was murmuring quietly or, like Sam, pretending to read. When the double doors that led to the operating room opened a few moments later, however, everyone
swiveled toward them as though pulled by a magnet.

Mrs. Goodman stood up when she saw the doctor come
out; this was apparently Dr. Patel, whom she had met before
the surgery. Any other time, Sam might have snickered at
what he was wearing. The blue gown and paper shoes weren't
too bad, but the funny-looking head covering — it looked
like a paper shower cap — added a comic note. Right now,
though, nothing was funny. Sam wasn't sure whether he
should join his mother or let her talk to the doctor alone, but
then Sam noticed that Dr. Patel was wearing a big smile, so he
hurried over.

"It was his spleen that had been damaged," explained the
doctor, "so we had to take it out. But not to worry. People
can survive quite well without a spleen."

The whole family was now gathered around Mrs. Goodman,
who asked, "And all the blood?"

"It looked much worse than it was. There was a head cut
that bled a good deal, but it was a surface wound."

"So he's going to be all right?" Ellen asked.

"I expect no complications, and a speedy recovery," Dr. Patel said, nodding happily.

"Yes!" Sam said, punching his fist in the air.

Everyone began hugging, even Nana and Grandma Sally, and Sam gave the thumbs-up sign to Mrs. Winters, who had been watching them anxiously from the volunteer desk. Then he went over to Dr. Patel and said, "Thanks . . . I . . ." Sam faltered. Dr. Patel shook his hand and gazed down on him with caring brown eyes. "Of course, of course, I'm so glad for all of you."

Happiness and relief blanketed Sam. He couldn't imagine ever feeling better than this.

Sam watched himself in his bedroom mirror as he tried to tie his tie. This was impossible. The knot was either too big, or the tie was left too short on one end and too long on the other.

Mr. Goodman appeared in the mirror over Sam's shoulder and turned him around by the shoulders. "Here, let me help you with that." As he arranged the tie properly, Mr. Goodman said, "So is Avi nervous?"

"He was plenty nervous yesterday. But I think he'll be fine. I've heard his speech twice, and he doesn't even use notes."

"There," Mr. Goodman said, patting the tie into place. "Now you look almost as good as me."

Sam grinned at his father. Mr. Goodman had been in a great mood ever since his "brush with death," as he called it. Mrs. Goodman told her husband not to joke about the accident, but he said it made him feel better to be able to laugh about it.

"Are you looking forward to the party after the service?" his father inquired.

"Sure," said Sam, though he didn't offer any further information. He was pleased that Heather had turned down the invitation to Avi's bar mitzvah. Though she hadn't given a reason, Avi thought perhaps it was because Sam and Heather had broken up. She was now seen everywhere with Robert Erlich, and acted as though Sam didn't exist and never had. Sam didn't enlighten Avi, but he preferred to think that Heather had realized it would have been hypocritical for her to show up at a bar mitzvah after the things she'd said to Sam. Whatever her reasons, it surprised him how little he cared.

Mr. Goodman walked over to Sam's desk and picked up the paper with the big red A on it. "This is the Holocaust paper?" he asked, scanning it.

"Yeah," Sam answered. He'd planned to show it to his parents, but had waited to savor the A privately for a day. In a way he was surprised by the grade. When it came to writing down what he'd learned about the Holocaust, it seemed he still had more questions than answers. But for some reason,

Mr. Tibold hadn't minded the uncertainties in his paper, and wrote in a note with the grade that Sam showed all the indications of an inquiring mind.

"I'd like to read this," Mr. Goodman said, putting it back down on the desk. "I have a feeling I can learn something from it."

Sam smiled. He was just happy to have his dad around to read his papers.

Ellen, who had come home for Avi's bar mitzvah after all, stuck her head inside Sam's doorway. "Come on, we're going to be late."

They still had plenty of time, but Ellen liked getting places early. So they followed her downstairs, where they found Mrs. Goodman dressed and ready to go, but peering at the calendar.

"Passover is a week before Easter this year," she said to her family, all of whom were now in the kitchen.

Sam groaned to himself. Did the Jewish and Christian holidays always have to march together two by two? Were things going to fall apart again, just when everyone seemed to be getting along so well?

Mrs. Goodman looked around. "I want us to have a seder for Passover this year."

"Are you sure?" Mr. Goodman asked.

"Mrs. Cohen is going to help me prepare it. We'll have the whole family, Nana and Grandma Sally, perhaps a few other relatives —"

No one made eye contact, and Pluto, who had been sitting quietly in the corner, got up and walked out of the room, nose held high, as if to say, "It's on your head, this time. I'm not getting involved." Finally, Maxie asked, "This isn't going to lead to trouble, is it?"

Everyone burst out laughing. That was one of Mrs. Goodman's favorite questions for her children.

"No," she said, giving Maxie a quick kiss on the top of his head. "It's something I want to do. I think your grand-mothers are ready, too. We all are. Besides, the last supper that Jesus went to was a Passover dinner, so in a way, this is part of my Easter holiday, too."

"And I think we should all go to Easter services this year," Mr. Goodman added. "I've gone to synagogue with my mother since my brush with death, but I want to say thank you to Whoever is up there in every religious building that I can."

Mrs. Goodman took her husband's hand.

"I don't get it," Maxie said, standing solemnly in his white shirt and bow tie. "Does this mean we're Jewish or we're Christian?"

"We're both," his father said. "We're mixed. I guess in this family it's going to be up to each one of us to decide what we believe and how we put those beliefs into practice."

"Maybe we could have done the religion thing differently," Mrs. Goodman said. "I'm sure some people think we've done it all wrong, but this is who we are."

Sam looked, really looked, at his family. He didn't see the different religions that sometimes came between them. He saw the one thing that held them together: love. It felt good, very good, to be Sam Goodman: part Jewish, part Christian, son, brother, grandson, and oh, yes, a kid on speaking terms with God.